By Kathleen Karr

The Cave

———

THE

CAVE

KATHLEEN KARR

Farrar Straus Giroux

New York

———

Library of Congress Cataloging-in-Publication Data
Karr, Kathleen.
The cave / Kathleen Karr.—1st. ed.
p. cm.
[1. Caves—Fiction. 2. Droughts—Fiction. 3. Farm life—South
Dakota—Fiction. 4. South Dakota—Fiction. 5. Depressions—1929—
Fiction.] I. Title.
PZ7.K149Cav 1994 [Fic]—dc20 94-9846 CIP AC

For Wes Adams—
A man of few words, but a master of many

The Cave

1

She woke hot and dry. She was always hotter and
drier after that dream. The one about water.
Enough water to grow some real crops on the family
spread. To keep down the dust that was always blowing,
getting into noses and eyes, giving the baby rashes,
keeping her younger brother, Michael, in endless fits of
asthma.

Water. She edged out of the double bed, careful not
to wake Michael, and groped blindly in the dark for the
water jug. She caught the baby's crib instead. He let
out a howl.

"Christine." Her mother's voice from beyond the curtain in the next room was tired.

"Yes, Ma?" A whisper.

"Settle the baby, honey?"

"Yes, Ma."

She picked up baby William and rocked him to her body, crooning softly. He groped for curves and, not finding enough, let out another howl. Christine sighed. "Won't find nothing there worth sucking at till you're way past sucking age, William." And she slid through the curtain to hand the baby to their mother, lying in bed with her nightgown unbuttoned, waiting.

"Sorry, Ma. I was thirsty."

"The whole world's thirsty, honey. Get me a little water, too?"

Christine finally found the water, took care of her mother, and carried her own glass outside the only door of the two-room shack. William's greedy, rhythmic gulps followed her into the night. Her father slept through it all.

Outside, the wind was still for once. And the sky clear, with the moon shining. She looked out toward the south, where the land went flat, her father's alfalfa struggling through an inch of loose dust that had blown up out of Nebraska. The Cheyenne River bounded their land, a thin, meandering strip that used to shine by the moon. Wasn't enough of a trickle left to catch the light.

She emptied her glass and, still thirsty, turned to the west, where the Black Hills began. They looked even more desolate in the moonlight, bald humps edging around the shack. Her eyes went back to the sky. Not a cloud in it, not even a dust cloud.

Christine had spent her twelve years learning how to read that sky at her father's side on this very land. There was no rain coming. She went back to bed.

Her father was under the old pickup out front the next morning. It was a '29 Ford, bought in the good days, now rusty and pockmarked from hard years on hard dirt roads.

"Aren't you going to plow up the kitchen garden today, Dad?"

"No point. Just loosen up more dust to blow around."

"I could water it from the well—"

"Hand me that spanner, daughter. I've been meaning to work on this axle anyway."

His mind was set. She bent to give him the tool. "Are we going into town?"

"Why? No money to spend."

Christine shrugged. "Just thought it might be something different."

"Haven't got enough gas to waste on something different. Go help your mother."

Christine scuffed her toes through the yard dust that used to be green grass, taking her time getting back to the kitchen. There'd only be the baby to diaper, and breakfast dishes to wash. It was always the same.

Her mother had already started on baby William. She glanced up from the table, where she was swabbing at his bottom, a safety pin in her mouth, a bobby pin holding back the bangs of her roughly trimmed blond hair. "Check on Michael?"

"Isn't he up yet?"

Her mother mouthed a no and Christine followed the sounds of coughing through the curtain divider. He was sitting against the pillows. He always looked so little, sitting propped up that way. More like five than eight years old.

"Want some porridge, Michael? I could bring you some."

He shook his head, and his voice came out wheezing: "I want something cold, Chrissie, and wet. Ice cream" —he stopped to catch his breath—"and an ocean of water, at least."

"Won't find any of them in South Dakota this year, Michael." She felt his narrow brow. It was hot and damp under his lank brown hair. "How about I get you a wet cloth?"

"If I can have a story with it. A wet story."

"Sorry. My stories all dried up, too. Just like these nineteen-thirties."

"Come on, Chrissie. Please."

She got him the cloth and arranged it on his head.

"Not now. I've got to think up one first. And, before that, I've got to do the dishes. Can you get up today? It's not blowing."

He shrugged, bony shoulders poking through his nightshirt. He was disappointed with her.

Christine left him for her chores. It was when she dropped a dish, and it broke, that her mother looked away from nursing William. "Was that my blue willow pattern?"

Christine was already down on her knees on the hard floorboards, picking up the shards. There were tears in her eyes. "I'm sorry, Ma. I didn't mean it!"

"That leaves only four from my mama's set."

Christine reached for a piece from under the table, right below the frayed hem of her mother's checked dress. "William can have mine when he's big enough for it."

"Christine?"

She swiped at her eyes. "Yes, Ma?"

"Take yourself a walk before you break another?"

"But the breadmaking—"

"I'll do it today. Take yourself a walk."

Christine got off her knees and put the pottery pieces on the table. "Maybe I can glue them back together."

Now her mother seemed like she might be ready to cry, too. Christine put an arm around her shoulder briefly, then ran for the door before Michael's coughing could drag her back. Outside, she ignored her father underneath the truck bed and raced up the nearest hill, the short skirt of her dress flapping behind her.

She ran for a long time, until there was hardly any breath left to run. Thistle and spiky yucca leaves scratched at her bare legs as she ran some more. Run out, she heaved up next to a bluff and slid down along its dried-grass face, feeling misery creeping through her entire body.

There'd be no kitchen garden to tend. That meant there'd be no vegetables for the summer, or to can for the winter. Michael was getting sicker every day. Her father looked to have given up. And her mother was ready to cry. She couldn't stand it when her mother cried. *She* could cry. That was all right. But when her mother cried, it seemed like the end of the world.

Christine scrabbled with her fingers in frustration at the rounded wall behind her back, groping for a chunk of rock big enough to throw at something. At anything. A piece broke away under her fingers and she turned to pick it up. It was a jagged hunk of stone. She grabbed it with both hands and pounded it back into the side of the hill. Earth broke away. Again and again she pounded, venting the furies inside her body.

Suddenly something gave.

Christine sat back on her haunches and examined her bloodied hands. Even the hills were turning to dust. Nothing but dust. She gave one final whack. The hill face crumbled in on itself, leaving a gap in its side.

A hole in a hill?

She edged closer. Chill, damp air rushed past her head, cooling the sweat running down her thin cheeks and nose, billowing her straw-colored hair. Christine picked up a rock shard and attacked the edges of the opening with every ounce of energy left in her. She heard a hollow echo of crumpling rubble, then pitched forward, through the rift.

It was dark inside, and blessedly cool. Christine lay prone for a long while, letting the coolness and the moisture spread over her body. When she finally pulled herself up, she ignored the aches starting in. She had to search for the pinprick of light that was her door out. It was a long way up. She'd probably be aching a lot worse if she'd known the distance and stiffened up for the fall. Strangely calm, she didn't scramble for the outside world. It hadn't much to offer at this moment. Instead, she stood fixed and listened.

There was a wind. Yes. But it was different from the prairie winds blowing from the north, or the mountain winds blowing from the west. Especially it was different from the dust winds blowing from the south.

There was something else, too. Her head turned to catch it. A soft, soothing, gurgling sound it was. Like water. Lots of water. As if being pulled, Christine walked toward the new sound. When she turned a bend, the pinprick of light from behind blinked out. She was left in a blacker darkness than she had ever known. Stock-still for a long moment, Christine finally backed around and found her light again. Bad luck ran in the family, but not stupidity.

It took three tries to scale the ragged walls to the entrance hole. She'd need a rope to fasten at the top and hang on to. And a lantern. She planned all the way back home.

2

H er father was still under the truck, her mother
 still in the kitchen, as if nothing had happened.
But the color of the sky had changed. It was turning
ugly black from the south.

"More dust coming, Ma!"

Her mother plopped a lump of dough into a pan and
swiped at her forehead. "I've got to get this bread in
the oven. See to wetting down the sheets and hanging
them around Michael, please. And maybe you'd better
ask your father to chase in the chickens and the mule."

"Yes, ma'am." Christine poked her head out the

screen door. "Dust coming again, Daddy! Mama says can you take in Big Ben and the chickens?"

A grunt came from under the truck.

"And, Daddy?"

His long legs inched out. "Yes?"

"You happen to have a piece of rope I could borrow? Say twenty feet long?"

The rest of him followed, lean and muscled and dust-covered from his shaggy brown hair to his heavy work boots. "What for?"

Christine considered. "Wanted to climb some rough sides up in the hills. Thought I saw animal tracks that way."

"Deer?" He was suddenly interested. A deer would feed them for a long time.

"Might be. Maybe even elk." An elk would feed them even longer.

"Check in the barn."

"Thank you!"

The dust storm came in the middle of the afternoon. It blocked out the entire sun, turning the day to twilight. Her mother and father were in the kitchen, stuffing rags at the edges of the closed windows, and under the door. It was stifling hot inside the little house.

The baby was napping, his crib draped in wet sheets to keep the dust down inside. Christine had made a tent around Michael, too, stringing the wet sheets on crisscrossed laundry line. Now she crawled in next to him. Already the breath came more harshly from his thin chest. He looked scared. Scared clear through his wide brown eyes.

Christine tried out a smile. "I thought up a story for you, Michael."

"What?"

She snuggled nearer and put her arm around his shoulders, pulling him close, even if it was hot. "Don't talk. Just listen. It's a secret story. Just for you. Understand?"

Those brown eyes sparked with a glint of gold as he nodded, blinking thick, dark lashes. Christine blinked her own paler ones in turn. How Michael had picked up all that color from their father beat her sometimes, when she just seemed to have washed-out leftovers from Mama, she and baby William both. Blue eyes not bright enough, hair not yellow enough, not even her mother's strong face—although it was a little too early to tell about that with William yet . . .

"You doing a story or not, Chrissie?"

"Hold your horses, Michael. You can't rush these things." She rearranged herself to get out from under those eyes. You couldn't rightly be jealous of someone as sickly as Michael. It wouldn't be fair. "OK, then. Here we go. Once upon a time . . ."

All their stories had to start with "Once upon a time." That was the way a good story, a story that could take you away from the dust, had to start.

"Once upon a time there was a girl and her little brother walking through the hills."

"Like our hills?"

"Yes, but greener. With trees all over. Trees filled with nuts to eat, and apples—the reddest, juiciest apples you ever sank your teeth into—and streams wandering around, filled with delicious fish. These fish were so fat and friendly you could just put your hand to the water and they'd jump into it, like they were itching to be done up in a pan with butter and flour and salt . . ."

Michael smiled at the thought.

"And that wasn't all, either. There were deer and elk everywhere. You practically tripped over them. There were so many you didn't have to hunt them. Besides, you were too full up on friendly fish, anyhow. So one day this sister and her little brother—"

"What were their names?" he breathed out.

"Chrissie and Michael. Like us." Their names were always Chrissie and Michael. That went along with the "Once upon a time." It had ever since Christine had started making up stories. That had been when the hard times set in, and the one-room schoolhouse down the way had closed, because the farmers and ranchers couldn't afford to pay for the teacher anymore. Three years now of drought. Michael just remembered their last teacher. He had been to school only a few months.

"One day Chrissie and Michael were following the most elegant stag, when suddenly he ran right up into the side of a hill and disappeared."

Michael's dark eyebrows rose at this impossibility.

"Well, naturally, they got curious, and had to follow."
She stopped. "What do you suppose they found?"

His whisper was hard to hear as the wind rose in
velocity around their walls, shaking them. "I can't . . .
can't figure it, Chrissie."

Christine reached out from under the tent for the
glass of water she'd left there. She pushed away the
scum of dust on its surface distastefully, then decided
to drink it off, so Michael wouldn't have to. They shared
the glass until it was empty.

"A cave, Michael. The most wondrous cave imaginable! With cool winds, and the sound, the feeling of
water. More water than we've ever seen or known."

He closed his eyes to consider her words, and soon
his head was lowered on her shoulder, resting. Beside
him, Christine closed her own gritty eyes, imagining
what she would find when she got back to the cave.
Her cave. The very first and only private thing in her
entire life.

It wasn't till two days later that Christine got her
chance. The dust from the storm had settled down into
rippled drifts, like sand on the edge of the ocean, her
mother said. Her mother had seen the ocean at a
moving-picture show.

Christine finished shoveling the dust away from the
two wooden steps up to the front door and paused to
brush limp pale hair from her shoulders, to rub a

smudge from her chin, to stare at the big *Orange Crush* sign painted on the side of the barn facing the dirt road. It had been up there since she could remember. The bright orange was beginning to flake off now, but it still made her want a soda pop awfully bad.

"Ma?"

"Yes, dear?" came from the vicinity of the stove inside.

"Be all right if I have a little walk in the hills? Maybe hunt for some early berries?"

"There won't be any, but I guess it wouldn't hurt to try. A few berries might put some color in Michael's cheeks."

"Thanks, Ma."

Christine carefully propped the shovel against the unpainted slats of the house and went to the barn, where her father was sieving dust from a tin can of gasoline.

"The tractor engine freeze up on you again, Dad?"

"Yup. Knew there was a reason God made mules."

"I'm just going to take that rope we talked about the other day, and a pail for berries?"

He was busy inspecting sediment in the layered cloth and didn't pay much attention. That way, she could take the extra lantern off the wall, too. Equipped, Christine took to the hills.

All the way she kept reminding herself where the hole was, hoping the storm hadn't hidden it. She passed three patches of wild strawberries before she remembered to inspect a fourth. It didn't matter. The berries were tiny, hard and white, looking like they'd never turn rosy. Then she stumbled over some spoor. She bent down to study the animal droppings. They were fresh, and too big for deer.

"I'll be." Christine glanced speculatively at the hills around her. "Wouldn't it be something if that little white lie of mine turned into truth."

At last she saw the hole. The entrance to the cave. Christine set down her empty pail and lantern. Working slowly and surely, she tied one end of her rope securely around a lone boulder just outside the mouth. She slung the loop of rope down the opening, already feeling the refreshing, cool dampness reaching for her. Christine paused only long enough to inspect the bright sky and pull a match from her pocket to light the lantern. Soon she was easing backward into the void, the handle of the lantern slung over one arm.

Hand over hand on the rope, feet groping for toeholds, she worked her way to the bottom. The rope was barely long enough. She had to jump the last few feet. But she was down, swinging the lantern around the space.

The entrance was not as large as she had remembered, but around the bend, where she had stopped before, a passage continued, taller than her head. Christine set down the lamp and groped in her pocket for the ball of string she'd thought to fetch along. Walking back to the entrance, she carefully tied an end to the dangling rope, then paid the line out behind her. There'd been a copy of *The Adventures of Tom Sawyer* in that one-room schoolhouse three years back. It had been dog-eared when she found it, and more so when she was finished with it. She wasn't about to get cave-lost.

It was a hefty ball of string, and it was only half used up when Christine stopped with a gasp. Before her, the passageway opened into an underground room. A big one. Stone icicles dangled down on all sides, wherever she swung the light from her lantern. But what stilled her breath was what flowed through the center of the room.

"A stream! Feeding right into a little pond!" she gasped.

It was only a few feet wide, that stream, but it flowed fast and sure from one darkened end of the chamber before merging into the still pool. Christine crept closer, till she was on its very brink. Carefully, so carefully, she set down the lantern, lowered her head, and tasted of the stream. It was cold and pure. She tried it with her fingers, then thrust in her arm. Something touched her in passing and she let out a little shriek. Other somethings jumped from the narrow waters as if unwilling to be hemmed in by its limits. Christine stared.

"Fish. Big fish. White."

The flicker of the lantern brought her back to reality. The kerosene was running low.

Plucking up the lantern, Christine dropped the ball of string by the stream and, following its lead, raced through the chamber and the passage. At the pinprick of light by the rope, the lantern died. She sank onto her knees, gasping.

"Thank you, Lord. Next time I'll see to filling the lantern."

The sky was dark with dust again when she got back to the house.

"Where's the pail, honey?"

"The pail? Sorry, Ma. I guess I left it at the last berry patch when I saw the sky. They weren't but hard little nuggets, anyway. Like stone."

"Close the screen door, Christine, and the winter door, too. We've got to stuff them."

"Yes, Dad." She closed the doors. "There *are* elk, Daddy. I found fresh spoor."

"If this dust ever stops, I'll take out the rifle. But it doesn't look to stop."

Christine went for the water jug. The liquid she poured was sandy and stale, not at all like the sweetness of her hidden stream. "Did you ever hear of white fish, Dad?"

"How do you mean?"

"Big white fish, more than a foot long. With funny eyes, almost blind."

Her father stopped fussing with rags long enough to stare up at her face. His brown eyes were wider than

Michael's, his cheeks already stubbly though he'd shaved this morning. Shaved every morning. "What goes on in that head of yours, daughter? You been sitting out in the hills making up stories again?"

"Maybe, Dad." Christine shifted uncomfortably to watch her mother stirring a pot at the stove. There were worry grooves in her forehead. "May I put some molasses on a slice of bread for Michael?"

"Take it easy on the molasses, Christine. The can's almost empty."

"I won't take any for myself, Ma."

Christine went to crawl into the bed-tent with Michael.

Their whispers came strangely clear through the howl of the wind.

"If I were to get better, to get up—"

"What then, Michael?"

"Could I see the cave? And the stream?"

"How do you know it's real, Michael? It could just be one of my stories. Like Dad says."

"Not this time, Chrissie."

"How do you know?" she insisted.

"I don't think you'd make up white blind fish. Any fish you'd make up, they'd be all colors of the rainbow. Like that trout used to run in the Cheyenne." He stopped for breath. "When Daddy took us fishing."

"You remember that, Michael? You must've been four last time we did that."

Plucking up the lantern, Christine dropped the ball of string by the stream and, following its lead, raced through the chamber and the passage. At the pinprick of light by the rope, the lantern died. She sank onto her knees, gasping.

"Thank you, Lord. Next time I'll see to filling the lantern."

The sky was dark with dust again when she got back to the house.

"Where's the pail, honey?"

"The pail? Sorry, Ma. I guess I left it at the last berry patch when I saw the sky. They weren't but hard little nuggets, anyway. Like stone."

"Close the screen door, Christine, and the winter door, too. We've got to stuff them."

"Yes, Dad." She closed the doors. "There *are* elk, Daddy. I found fresh spoor."

"If this dust ever stops, I'll take out the rifle. But it doesn't look to stop."

Christine went for the water jug. The liquid she poured was sandy and stale, not at all like the sweetness of her hidden stream. "Did you ever hear of white fish, Dad?"

"How do you mean?"

"Big white fish, more than a foot long. With funny eyes, almost blind."

Her father stopped fussing with rags long enough to stare up at her face. His brown eyes were wider than

1 9

Michael's, his cheeks already stubbly though he'd shaved this morning. Shaved every morning. "What goes on in that head of yours, daughter? You been sitting out in the hills making up stories again?"

"Maybe, Dad." Christine shifted uncomfortably to watch her mother stirring a pot at the stove. There were worry grooves in her forehead. "May I put some molasses on a slice of bread for Michael?"

"Take it easy on the molasses, Christine. The can's almost empty."

"I won't take any for myself, Ma."

Christine went to crawl into the bed-tent with Michael.

Their whispers came strangely clear through the howl of the wind.

"If I were to get better, to get up—"

"What then, Michael?"

"Could I see the cave? And the stream?"

"How do you know it's real, Michael? It could just be one of my stories. Like Dad says."

"Not this time, Chrissie."

"How do you know?" she insisted.

"I don't think you'd make up white blind fish. Any fish you'd make up, they'd be all colors of the rainbow. Like that trout used to run in the Cheyenne." He stopped for breath. "When Daddy took us fishing."

"You remember that, Michael? You must've been four last time we did that."

"They were beautiful." He coughed. "Tasted beautiful, too. I remember."

Christine considered as baby William's howl joined in with the wind's. She'd discovered the cave. It would still be hers, even if she shared it with her brother.

"If you get yourself strong enough to walk up into the hills with me, Michael, I'll show you."

"Hand me that bread and molasses, Chrissie. I've got to eat more to get strong enough."

She fished under the sheet tent and her fingers settled on a gooey blob. "It's going to have dust on it."

"Dust has to be good for something." Michael bit into it.

The wind had died down, and over the sounds of Michael's belabored breathing Christine listened to her parents talking in the next room.

"What if I took Big Ben into town, Clarise? Tried to sell him. I can't keep him in oats much longer."

"But the tractor isn't working. And if the rains come, Ernest—"

Christine heard her father's big hand slam onto the tabletop. "It's been three years! Three years of drought, this year worse than the last two. The rains aren't coming."

He said that last so hopelessly Christine shivered.

"What to do, then, Ernest? . . . What to do?"

"We might have to leave."

There was only silence from her mother.

Leave. Leave her father's land that had been his father's? That his grandfather had homesteaded? Where would they go? The wind came up again, and Christine could hear no more. She closed her eyes.

3

———————

Michael made an effort. He forced down more food than he'd stomached for weeks. He left the bed and walked, haltingly at first around the room and into the kitchen, and then out to the back yard. After a week of this, during which their mother took heart from Michael and occasionally began to hum around her pots, Christine felt it was time for action. Michael wasn't anywhere strong enough yet to take on the hills, but if she waited too long he might give up. She left her brother sitting in the sun on the bench outside the door to confront her mother.

"Ma?"

"Yes, dear?" Mama stopped her stitching at a new outfit for baby William, who'd already crawled holes through his two long shirts.

"The sky looks clear, and it's not too hot?"

"What's on your mind, Christine?"

"Michael's doing so well I thought maybe a walk in the hills . . ."

"He's not near ready for the hills yet, honey."

"It'd be a kind of reward. To keep him working. And I'd help."

"Seems to me you've already had something to do with all this," her mother said. Crisp blue eyes searched Christine's face. "I'm not sure exactly what, either." Her eyes slid back to the needle. "But when you're good and ready, you'll tell me."

"May we, Ma? You won't be sorry."

The stitching stopped again. "Be careful. Please. He's so frail—"

Christine was already out the door, bending over Michael, whispering. "If you can do it, I'll take you to the cave."

His face lit up and he was on his feet.

"Not so fast. It's a long way."

It was longer than Christine remembered. She almost gave up several times. Michael was wheezing too hard, gasping for air. But each time she tried to turn him around he fought her and struggled forward over the next mound of hill.

Reaching the hole at last, she lit the lantern and took it down first. She returned to sling Michael on her back, carrying him below with effort. At the bottom she pried his fingers from her neck and eased him to the floor.

"Can you hear it? Smell it?"

Michael's chest rattled from the effort. With a cough, he cleared it. He breathed slowly, not believing the new ease of it.

"Chrissie," he whispered. "The air is different here. It doesn't hurt!"

"Rest a minute. It's even better inside."

"No." He struggled up. "I want to see that water *now*."

They sat by the stream for ages, feet dangling in the rushing wetness. It was somehow more interesting than the small, flat pond just beyond, whose edges disappeared into the waiting darkness of the room. Michael began to laugh.

"What's so funny?"

"Your blind fish. They tickle when they go by. And one of them nibbled on my toes."

Christine groaned. "I knew I forgot something! I meant to bring a pole, and one of Daddy's hooks. Even meant to root for some worms. It all just vanished from my head—clean out of it, when we set out so fast."

"Doesn't matter, Chrissie. I don't think I'd like to eat these fish anyway."

" 'Cause of how funny they look?"

"No. Because they make me happy."

Christine stared at her brother through the dim lantern light. He hadn't wheezed in over an hour, she was sure. And he was talking all the way through his thoughts, not stopping for extra breaths. "Maybe you're right. Maybe these *are* special fish. Holy."

"Like in church?"

"Sort of, but even more so." Christine took in the fragile icicles, hundreds of them gracefully decorating the chamber over their heads, haloed by the lantern's soft glow. "Maybe this whole place goes back to the beginning of everything . . . to the creation of the world."

Michael grinned. "And God was saving it all this time just for us."

Christine eased back on her elbows and pulled her chilled feet from the water. "Why not? Why not save it for those who truly need it?" There was a fair amount of water down here. And not nearly enough up there, outside. It must be good for something. And if anyone truly needed it, it was she and Michael and their father . . . "If we were to get a pump down here, and water pipes—"

"Daddy could irrigate again! Like he does when the Cheyenne's running!"

"But it would take miles of pipes, Michael. Miles of pipes, and Daddy's only got a few. Not to mention the gas it would use up, running a proper pump. Then again . . ." She studied the stream in a new way, calculating what it might hold. "Then again, it's a fairly small stream. And it sort of dead-ends into that little pool. Don't think it would be enough to make a difference." She shook her head with regret. "No. It would only upset him more . . . seeing something he needs so badly, but hardly enough to whet his appetite. It'll just make him hungry for more." She sighed. "Best leave it be."

"You sure about that, Chrissie?"

"Certain sure."

It was accepted. Michael was fairly used to his sister's certain sureness. He hauled out his own legs and Christine bent to wipe them with her skirt. She was waved away as he rolled down his overall cuffs. "I can do it myself, Chrissie."

"So you can." She smiled.

In silent agreement, the two followed the string back through the tunnel. Only now Christine began to notice other smaller openings hiding between rare sparks of glitter that her lantern beams picked out on the walls. There were other holes leading to other passageways, perhaps other rooms. They would explore them all when Michael was well enough.

When they returned, Mama was sitting on the back steps with baby William hanging onto her skirt where it fell just below her knees, practicing at pulling himself up. She tried to hide the relief on her face.

"You certainly took a long walk."

"We sure did," Michael said with a grin. He plunked himself down next to their mother.

"You look different, child, besides the color in your cheeks. What did you see in the hills?"

"Wonders, Mama—"

"The wonders of nature," interrupted Christine smoothly. "Found two strawberries actually come ripe enough to eat. And more spoor. Daddy really ought to take out his gun. A little venison'd go a long way toward making up for no molasses."

Their mother slowly turned her head between the two of them, shaking it as if she knew full well nothing more would be forthcoming. "The day's almost gone, Christine. Help me with the meal?"

"Sure thing, Ma."

After supper Daddy lifted his hunting gun from its hooks on the wall high over the door frame. Christine hurried to gather the dishes to give him space for the expected ritual. Michael, still at table for the first time in weeks, pushed himself up to fetch the gun oil and clean rags wedged behind the soup bowls on a kitchen shelf.

Daddy noticed with a slightly raised eyebrow. "Thank you, son."

Michael beamed, hid a small cough, and sank back into his chair.

"Wrong time to go hunting," Daddy commented as he carefully broke open the muzzle and verified the two chambers were, indeed, empty. "It ought to be in the autumn, when the young ones can fend for themselves." He oiled a piece of rag and screwed it into a chamber. "Hope it's a buck you've been trailing, Christine."

Christine turned away from the dry sink, where she'd been scrubbing at the dishes. "Has to be, Daddy. It was big spoor."

Mama pushed through the curtains from the back room and lowered herself into a chair, waving her apron at her face. "William finally gave up for the day, kicking to the end." Her eyes traveled the table and over to her daughter finishing the dishes. A smile built on her face, easing out the recent worry lines. "What a blessing to have us all together again."

Daddy shoved some cotton up the second chamber and grunted.

Christine woke before the dawn to muffled sounds from the front room. She poked her head through the curtain.

"Going after that buck now, Dad?"

He put a finger to his lips. Mama was still curled up in the big bed by the far wall.

Christine smoothed wrinkles from her cotton nightgown. "If I were to go with you," she whispered, "it might help."

Her father shook his head no.

"Might be I could guide you, Dad," she tried again.

"I know where the spoor lies." Near the cave. She wouldn't guide him there, only close enough. If that cave had been left for her and Michael, surely there'd be a little of the gift flowing out. Just enough for Daddy to bag himself a nice elk.

"Please, Daddy."

His eyes came up from the bread he was wrapping in a big red handkerchief. He studied Christine. Then he picked up the bread knife and started cutting another slice.

Christine didn't waste any time on gratitude. She slipped through the curtains to pull on her dress and a sweater.

The air outside had a difference to it. Unable to accept that difference after all this time, Christine stood in it, sniffing. Behind her, to the east, the faintest light crept onto the high plains.

"Is it mist, Dad?"

He was already striding off to the west. She raced to catch up. "Is it mist? And will it help?"

"Can't hurt. But it won't help enough."

"Stands to reason, Daddy"—she was half jogging to keep up with his long legs—"stands to reason it's got to rain sometime."

"Doesn't rain in the next three weeks, it won't matter anymore. It'll be too late."

"Is that what we've got, Dad? Three weeks?"

Her father hesitated long enough to wipe the cool

moisture from his face with a shirtsleeve. "Sometimes you act much younger than your twelve years, girl. Dancing along after me, asking silly questions. You know the answer near as well as I do. I taught you to know . . . After three weeks the growing season will be too short—and the sprouts already up burnt out."

Christine ignored the insult. The mist had just made her a little frisky. Three weeks for a miracle. She changed their course slightly, toward the cave.

When her father's heavy work boots squished into fresh, steaming spoor, he didn't fuss. He unshouldered his gun.

Christine felt the light breeze blowing early-morning cool on her face. It was coming from the right direction, away from the game. That buck, if he truly existed, wouldn't smell them. Not yet. He'd take notice, though, if they made any untoward noise. She consciously stepped toe first, cringing as the dried grasses crinkled beneath her weight. Would that be enough of a sound? Too much sound?

Concentrating as she was, she almost didn't notice where the spoor was taking them—nearly to the mouth of her secret. It was just beyond the next hillock. Surely Daddy would spot it. It'd be hard to miss that telltale rope wound around the biggest boulder in sight, or the gaping mouth opening into blackness.

Christine stopped dead, torn between her family's need for food and a stronger need to keep the cave hers, at least until she figured out her reasoning—beyond just the stream that couldn't possibly help . . . She'd felt so positive of that. Could she be wrong? What if they were to try another tack, maybe cobble together a treadmill and set Big Ben to it? Wouldn't any gasoline be used up that way. But there still wouldn't be enough pipes to carry the water, and Big Ben would likely keel over dead from the exertion, as old as he was getting.

She swayed in her tracks, still figuring. Then again, if Daddy were to borrow enough pipes from enough neighbors . . . But most of the neighbors were ranchers and made do with a few windmills to water their stock. There probably wasn't enough pipe in the entire state to reach that stream. And not enough water to justify the effort once it was reached. Fairly certain again, Christine raised a foot as her father, with no compunctions holding him back, moved methodically, relentlessly forward.

Moments before all would be discovered, Christine glanced to the north. "Dad!" she sighed with relief.

He spun, rifle cocked, and aimed. A glorious buck stood silhouetted in the first red rays of the sun just above them, just above her cave, where passageways wandered dark and hidden beneath. Frozen between fears, Christine's attention sped to her father's fingers. She watched them tighten on the trigger. She heard the gun spit, once. The buck faltered slightly before sprinting for the north. Christine and her father followed the trail of blood, away from the cave.

They found the animal lying on its side beneath the only cover in sight. It was an ancient jack pine, with gnarled roots grasping deep into the earth for the moisture denied it on the surface.

"He's still alive, Dad. Do you need to use the other shell?"

"No. I'm running short on shells. Turn away, Christine."

Christine turned as her father groped for his knife. She held her breath a long minute.

"It's all right now, daughter. Go fetch Big Ben and the cart."

"Yes, sir." But she hesitated.

"What is it now, Christine?"

"Seems kind of a shame. He was so elegant—"

"God gave us dominion over all the earth, girl, and over every living thing that moves upon the earth. A man would be a fool not to take advantage of what's still left of it."

Christine didn't look back again. She wanted to remember the buck as she'd first seen him, so proud and alive above her secret place.

Daddy had the tiny smokehouse fired up for the first time in ages. Mama had elk ribs in the oven, and Christine was helping her grind meat to make sausages. They'd already eaten the liver for their midday meal. Michael had eaten so much that he'd climbed into bed for a nap, from repleteness rather than exhaustion.

Even baby William had eaten his share, mashed. Now he was crawling in circles around the kitchen, faster than ever. Amazing what a good meal could do.

"How far you figure this meat will take us, Mama?"

"Weeks, Christine. Maybe even months if we're careful. Maybe until something grows."

"You mean until the rain, Ma."

Her mother shoved another hunk of meat and fat into the funnel of the grinder. Her washed-out blue sleeves were rolled way above her elbows and her lower arms glistened with elk fat. "The Lord brought us food, Christine. Surely He has a little water somewhere?"

Christine opened her mouth as if to say something, then shut it again. Mama grabbed at baby William before he started practicing his exercises on the hot stove.

Daddy was the only one not bucked up by his catch. Christine found him by the woodpile, splitting logs to feed all the fires he had going. She stood well out of his way as he hefted the ax, then rammed it into the wood with passion. Chips scattered in all directions.

"Looks like you and the truck are needing a trip to the far hills for more wood, Dad. Since you chopped down near every blessed tree in the vicinity."

"Yup." *Thwack*.

"You worrying about sparks from the smokehouse catching onto the dry grass?"

"Maybe." *Thwack*.

"I can keep a lookout for you with the shovel. Ma

and I got the sausage all stuffed. Meantime, let me get you another armful of wood."

Christine went to the far end of the pile to dislodge a log. It was fairly spindly. Probably the last of the cottonwood from down along the Cheyenne. She did miss seeing them bend with the wind along the river bed, a long, shady row of silvery-green life. Daddy'd cut those trees without a thought when they'd been needed. He probably figured it was all part of his duty to subdue and dominate the earth. At least his piece of it.

She shook visions of living trees from her head to concentrate on extracting the cottonwood limb without all the rest toppling onto her bare feet. She also spared a thought as to why her father wasn't happier with his day's work. And hers, too. She *had* led him to the right place, after all. Things just seemed to be possible around her cave. Even the elk had done his share, acting as a decoy, sacrificing his life—as if it were all meant to be. She gave another tug, then let out a little shriek.

"Daddy!"

He came at the run and saw what had her frozen in place. It was a rattler, head raised, forked tongue at the ready.

"Move! Now!"

Christine moved.

Thwack.

When Christine opened her eyes, her father was dangling the six-foot serpent from his fist. "Toss it in the smokehouse, daughter. It'll be good food when the elk runs out."

Christine gulped. "OK if I take the rattle first, Dad?"

"Just don't show your mother. She's been skittish about snakes since she found that one hissing from her fry pan last summer."

"Yes, sir. No, sir."

Thwack. Daddy was back at the firewood. Just like that.

Christine had to stand lookout by the smokehouse for two days past the dressing of the elk, bashing at stray sparks until the meat was ready and the banked fire could be extinguished. It was a lonely job, but practically everything out here was lonely since the drought.

She thought a lot about how much she missed school. Most of her classmates had considered it just another chore, but Christine had gloried in her teacher, in the few books, in the possibilities that came from brand-new ideas. She longed for Miss Cleanthe Smith and the books more than for the company of the other children. Only book they had around the house was the family

Bible, and that was mostly tucked away these days to keep it from the dust. Tucked along with it seemed to be her father's mealtime graces, too. Christine missed his quiet pleading to the Almighty for rain. Even that had dried up.

And there'd been church socials and dances back in those old days. How her mother and father had relished those dances. Sometimes there'd be fiddles, and sometimes an old Victrola cranked up, its needle skimming over records. She'd been too young yet to join in, but it had been fun watching her parents fox-trot and two-step around the Grange Hall in town, laughing, not worrying.

Christine wanted the fun and laughter back. She wanted to see her father's eyes filled with mischief as he swooped her mother around the dance floor, making her a girl again. She wanted him looking young and eager as he headed out to his fields in the morning, a whistle on his lips. She wanted her mother singing full out loud over her pots, or grinning as she schemed over the ingredients of the once-in-a-lifetime pie that would win her a blue ribbon at the County Fair.

But mostly Christine was hungry for fresh ideas. Maybe that's why the cave was so special. Its possibilities were becoming endless in her mind, an endless book with more pages always ready to be turned. And they were *her* pages. Hers to work out the end of the story. Well, hers with a little help from Michael.

And Michael still seemed better after the smokehouse fire was out, better enough to badger her about taking him back. She'd meant to anyway, proof being the slim stick she'd been fussing with during her vigil. She handed it to him.

"What's this for?"

"To help you over the hills, Michael."

He stopped to inspect it just beyond the barn. "It's got a nice heft, all right, Chrissie. But no way am I gonna carry a crutch like a cripple." Dark eyes flashing displeasure, he waved the rod in the air as if to sling it off into the nearest gully.

"Whoa. Wait! It's not any kind of a crutch, Michael. It's a *walking stick*. It's also something else, something mighty particular."

He paused, dubious. "Well, you did polish the knob at the top nice."

"Look closer, Michael."

He held it nearer. "What're these marks for, down the side?"

"It's a calendar, starting with the day Daddy bagged the elk."

"What do we need a calendar for? Mama's got that one up in the kitchen, from the funeral parlor in Hot Springs."

"That's two years old, Michael. She only leaves it up for the pretty pictures. You know she's got a soft spot for Hot Springs. This is to keep track of the time left before it rains. I couldn't do it in the house without Mama and Daddy asking questions."

Michael touched the careful grooves. "You've got three days marked here. How many you figure before the rain comes?"

"Daddy said three weeks." Three weeks and the waiting would be over, one way or the other. Not much reason to point that out. "Twenty-one days. How many does that leave, Michael?" She watched his brow furrow as he worked backwards in his head from twenty-one.

"Eighteen? The rain will come in eighteen days?"

"Or before," Christine answered positively. "Let's not waste any more time getting to the cave. You need to be strong when the rain starts. I'll be expecting help with planting the garden."

Michael gripped the staff and set off. "Carrots and turnips and potatoes, all right, Chrissie. I'm getting hungry for some. But I'm not wasting time planting any of those flowers of yours. You want flowers, *you* plant them. I'll be too busy helping Daddy with the alfalfa and wheat and oats. That's a *man's* work."

Christine grinned. At this rate, Michael would be strong enough to fight with soon. Then she'd let him know about man's work and woman's work.

The cave was waiting for them, welcoming. At the bottom of the rope, Christine adjusted the lantern's wick and set off down the main passage.

"I do believe I've missed it. It feels like coming

home." Unconsciously hurrying, she was already halfway to the big room. "Michael? You tuckered and need to rest? . . . Michael! Where are you?"

His voice came hollowly from behind and to the left. "Chrissie! I'm stuck. I took a wrong turn—"

Christine retraced her steps till she arrived at one of the smaller tunnels she'd been ignoring. "Michael! You can't just run off like that!" Swinging the lantern inside the passageway, she saw him. "You little stinker. You snuck one of Mama's candles! And a match!"

"Some yarn, too." He chuckled, gesturing with his flickering candle toward a small ball abandoned at his feet. "I've been thinking on it since you first brought me here, Chrissie. Thinking on how I'd like to discover something, too. *Michael's Room*." He tested the sound and apparently liked it.

Christine felt anger building but stomped it back. Getting angry with her brother would just set him off to worse mischief. She knew he had it in him. He'd been a regular little demon before the drought and the asthma. "That does sound fine, Michael. But caving can't be done alone. It has to be thought out, and we have to protect each other so nothing happens. There could be holes, cracks to fall into . . ." Her voice went very firm. "We need to do it *together*, Michael."

His small rebellion seemed to be dying down, particularly since he was still jammed into the tight crevice. His body was already twisted sideways, and small as he was, he couldn't go farther down this particular tunnel. "Maybe you're right, Chrissie. How about pulling me out?"

"Not yet." She carefully set down the lantern. "First you're going to swear to me. Swear that you'll never do this again . . . Or I'll never bring you again."

"Then you'll be in the cave by yourself. You just said—"

"I'd only go into the big room, Michael. And you'd be missing that. And the fish."

He considered. "All right. I swear."

"Not just like that. You have to swear on something special."

"What?"

Christine closed her eyes and breathed in the cool, moist air surrounding them. "Swear on the cave, Michael. The sacredness of the cave. And the rain."

Michael was becoming uncomfortable. His candle was dripping hot wax down the free arm that held it. "I swear, already. On the rain and the cave, that we only explore together. Is that it, Chrissie? 'Cause if it is, catch this candle. It's going to fall sure as I'm stuck."

Christine ran for the candle and efficiently dislodged Michael, shoving him behind her. Next she thrust the candle through the hole he'd been occupying. "Not much in there anyway. Only a small space with red walls and a flat dirt floor." She pulled out the candle and her head.

"Let me look, too!"

"All right, if you don't believe me."

"It's got nothing to do with not believing you. I just want to see." Finally satisfied, he turned to his sister. "What's next?"

"Why don't you pick another tunnel, Michael? I'll let you go first. That way it'll be *your* room when you find something."

"Truly?" Suspicion entered his voice. "You aren't trying to trick me?"

"Never in the cave, Michael. Really and truly."

Michael proceeded with more discretion. He refused three tunnels before he finally chose one. Decided, he led the way boldly for maybe fifty yards—as boldly as possible, stooped all the while beneath a lowering ceiling of rock. Christine followed, almost on her knees. She was beginning to wonder how Mama could possibly miss the fresh dirt and tears on Michael's overalls and her dress, when Michael, feet wriggling behind, disappeared before her eyes. She scurried on all fours—lantern dragging—to the hole where he was last seen. She poked the lantern tentatively through the hole.

"Michael?"

His voice came back gasping, but from excitement. "It's mine, Chrissie! *Mine!*"

Christine inched through the hole, feet first, and finally felt a welcome solidness beneath her. Only then did she look.

"Oh! Michael!"

His room was small but exquisite. Their lights glinted from every surface, revealing a wonderland of frosty crystals, tiny balls of popcorn, and in the center, a snow-covered Christmas tree. It was all white, blindingly white. And it was all so fragile Christine was afraid to move. "Don't touch anything, Michael—"

She was too late. He'd touched the Christmas tree and one fine crystalline needle fell, tinkling on the rock below. Michael stared, then burst into tears.

Christine reached for him. "It's all right, Michael. It's only one needle."

"But it was so perfect!"

"The room is still almost perfect. That one fallen needle will make it yours. Just don't cough in here. Please."

Michael pulled himself together. "Let's go to the water, Chrissie. I need to rest."

Christine found her handkerchief for him. *She* needed to think.

"Just a minute, Chrissie." Michael halted outside the tunnel leading to his discovery. "There are so many holes here, I might never find my room again. Could I leave a mark somewhere? So I remember? Would it be all right?"

"We don't have anything for writing, Michael. But then again . . ." She considered the candle still smoking in his hand, leaving a smutty trail in the air. "Let me try something with that candle."

He handed it over and watched as Christine held the

flame close to the hard rock surface of the wall at the tunnel's edge. Slowly, she worked out the letter "M" in black soot.

"Let me have that!" Michael grabbed the candle from her hand to make the mark of a small arrow pointing inward. "There," he said with satisfaction. "My room marked forever."

"Yes. I'm afraid so."

Their feet were dangling in the stream again, and Christine was doing her hard thinking. Up to this point they'd left no permanent sign of their coming into this place. Now, of a sudden, there was a broken crystal and a soot-smudged wall. Was this what happened when God allowed people into His secrets? Is that what'd happened at the Garden of Eden the minister was always going on about when they had enough gas to go into town for church? The perfect slowly became less perfect.

What would happen if others knew about her cave? They'd be leaving footprints where none had been. Worse still, they'd be touching things, taking little samples of those crystals and popcorn in Michael's room. Maybe even the icicles gloriously hovering above the stream. It was irresistible, the need to touch, to take, to change things. Even perfect things.

"Michael?"

"What?"

"You remember when our teacher used to talk about

how the land outside used to be? When it was just Indians and elk and buffalo?"

"Not hardly."

"Miss Cleanthe Smith used to say the dust never blew back in those days. The grass just grew taller and taller, without the plows stopping it, messing it up. And there were buffalo everywhere. Millions of them."

"Wouldn't ever go hungry then, would we, Chrissie?"

"I guess not. Maybe the Indians didn't."

"What happened to all the Indians?"

"There's still a few around. But I think maybe we chased most of them away, like the buffalo."

"*We* didn't do any chasing. Not Daddy and Mama and us."

"No, not us. But the people before us. People from the East. Maybe even Daddy's grandfather."

Michael pulled his toes out. "The fish don't seem to be tickling today . . . What brought on this Indian business, Chrissie?"

"The cave. Finding your room. Marking it . . ." Christine made a sudden decision. It was a decision she'd been waltzing around for days, at first just to keep something private for herself. Now it wasn't selfish any more. It finally made sense. "I don't think I'm ever going to let anybody else in, Michael."

"Not even Mama and Daddy and baby William when he's big enough?"

"Maybe William . . . Oh, I don't know." She stared up at the perfect icicles dangling overhead. "Mama would maybe understand, I think. I hate not telling her. It could make her happy."

"Wouldn't that be good, Chrissie? Making Mama happy?"

"It would be wonderful. But it couldn't stop there. It wouldn't. I just know it. Grownups have trouble with secrets—"

"How long till you'll be a grownup, Chrissie?" he interrupted, genuinely concerned.

"Not for a while, Michael. I don't think I'm ready for it yet. Ready for the way they never say anything outright, but you can see it on their faces."

"Like when Mama worries about me and the asthma? She doesn't say anything. But it's written all over her. Just like a book."

"Like that. Or Daddy and the rain."

Michael coughed for the first time since they'd entered the cave. "It might all be worth it, though. Just to see the light in Mama's eyes."

Christine bent to drift her fingers through the water. "It might at that, Michael."

5

There were six notches on the counting stick when the lightning began. It started at sunset, the strokes flashing electricity across the darkening sky. The family had been finishing dinner, and they all rushed out to watch.

Daddy stood twitching almost as bad as the sky, probably trying to figure if the bolts had any rain behind them. Mama twisted and wrung at her apron till Christine was sure she'd have it in shreds. Michael was swinging the counting stick gleefully, clearly convinced it would need no new marks carved upon it. Christine hung onto baby William. She had trouble hearing the distant thunder over his frightened shrieks.

A fresh bolt crackled, bringing Mama and Daddy both back to reality. Standing in their sheltered gully between the hills, they stared at the hot, black scar the lightning had made upon a nearby hummock of dry grass. Within seconds, fire flared around it. The orders came as fast.

"Put William in his crib, Christine."

"Yes, Ma."

"Then get to the water pump and start working it. Michael and I will go for the hose and pails."

"Yes, Dad."

Christine didn't need to ask why. She dumped the squalling baby in safety and ran to the well. Lightning without rain was disaster. That small stretch of fire would be eating up the dry prairie in another few minutes. They'd have to wet down the roof of their house, and the wall slats, too. Next, they'd have to go after the barn and the outbuildings.

As she hung on to the pump handle, jerking up and down with it to fill the trough, Daddy was already rigging up his one lone piece of hose to a small gas-powered pump and aiming the nozzle at the house.

Michael brought and filled pails and Mama sloshed off with them to dash the precious water at their home. Christine kept pumping into the trough until she knew with a certainty her arms would fall off. Then she pumped some more, afraid to glance at the burning hill. Afraid to stop long enough to test the wind.

Not until her mother spelled her did Christine chance a look. Thank the Lord, the wind was blowing the other way, to the west. It was blowing away from their home, away from Daddy's stunted fields. It was blowing toward her cave. Daddy noticed the change, too. He turned off the hose.

"Can't waste any more water here. Wet some empty feed sacks in the trough, daughter. I'll get shovels. We'll have to go after the edges of the burn."

"Me, too, Dad!" yelled Michael.

That halted their father for a moment. "*Not* you, too. You're nowhere near strong enough." Michael's excitement wilted. "You're in charge of the baby. Keep him safe so your mother can help. Our lives are more important than anything else."

"More important than the rain, Dad?"

"The rain won't help if we're dead, son."

"Well, it could sure help put out this prairie fire. Then we wouldn't be in danger at all."

Christine watched their father stoop to slosh his head in the water trough. She followed suit right next to him, and just managed to catch his last words as he shook his head like a wet dog.

"There are all different kinds of danger in life, Michael. We won't ever be free from every one of them."

With her father in the lead, Christine and her mother spread out to either side, stomping and swatting and killing the edges of the burn, coughing deep down in their chests worse than Michael as the smoke took to their lungs. Always the fire raged ahead of them, eating up the land.

A good mile over the hills—outlined in the night by the blaze—they saw other bent figures working through the smoke toward them. When they met, Daddy sent Mama back home. Christine stayed. She hadn't seen neighbors in so long she was hungry for their voices.

Funny how prairie fires turned into social events in these parts. Mr. Rasmussen was already lighting up his pipe, in spite of the thick haze surrounding them all. His red beard and face were black with soot. Christine rubbed at her own cheeks, but the hand she brought away was too dirty to tell if she'd helped or hindered her appearance. The hand burned, too, from the tiny sparks that had singed it. She tried licking at a piece of raw skin.

"Got the steers moved out in time, Ernest, but this ain't gonna help their grazing possibilities."

"We get any rain, Red, the grass should come back stronger than ever."

Another neighbor, Frank Finley, swiped at his face with a handkerchief before peering at the sky. "I can't tell with this smoke haze, but it don't look good. If nothing breaks the next two weeks, me and my family's pulling out."

Christine remained silent in the background, unconsciously nursing her hand, waiting for her father's question. She knew what it would be.

"Where to, Frank? Where's better?"

"California. Just pack 'em all up in the Chevy and we'll be gone."

Slowly the smoke-shrouded figures parted, each beating a new path across the prairie. Her father seemed to notice Christine for the first time.

"Get yourself home, daughter."

"I can still help, Daddy."

"It's past midnight. Get home before I have to carry you."

It was while her mother was lathering lard on her burned hands and arms the next morning that Christine had an idea. She waited until the strips of rag bandaging were in place.

"Looks like the three of us cleaned out the lard bucket, Ma."

"We certainly did. I'm thankful I saved up that rendered fat from the elk. Else there'd be nothing to cook with."

"May I have the empty bucket, Ma? For carrying things?"

"I don't see why not."

Christine picked up the wire handle awkwardly. "I feel like one of those mummies Miss Cleanthe Smith told us about once, all wrapped up like this." Dangling the bucket in front of her, she turned on Michael, who'd been jealously watching their mother's ministrations.

"*Beware the mummy's curse!*"

Michael jumped and Mama sighed. "Wherever did you get that imagination, Christine? I just don't know sometimes."

"From the prairie winds, Ma. Winds coming from deep beneath the prairie earth." She just managed to snatch the can opener behind her mother's back and trotted out the door with her booty.

Christine felt good that morning, even aching all over as she was. The hills to the west were black instead of dun-colored, but her family still had their house, and her father's grain still struggled through the dust all the way down to the Cheyenne. There were yet two weeks for the rains to come. Christine disappeared behind the barn to work on her lard bucket.

When Michael found her half an hour later, she was admiring her creation. Her head jerked up at his cough.

"The smoke didn't help your asthma."

"Never mind that," he wheezed. "What are you up to?"

"Find me a candle and I'll show you."

Michael trudged off to hunt for one. He returned flourishing it. "Ma caught me. She wanted to know what it was for."

"What did you tell her?"

"The truth. It was for your invention."

"Fair enough." Christine poked the candle through the opening she'd laboriously cut in the bucket's side. "Now watch." She speared the candle upright onto a waiting nail. It lodged there firm and straight.

"So?"

"So, dummy, I've made you a cave lantern. You won't have to burn yourself next time. So your hands don't end up mummified, like mine. Also, the shiny insides of the can will reflect the light. It'll be much brighter."

"Oh. Say—" Michael brightened. "Thanks, Chrissie! When can we go try it?"

"Not today. Might still be fire-hot up that way. We'll have to be patient."

Michael kicked at the dirt. "Don't want to be patient. I'm fed up with being patient. Been patient in bed seems like forever. Now there's finally something to get excited about, I want to do it. And I need some of that air, too."

Christine knew he needed some of that air. "Stop kicking up the dust, Michael. It won't help anything. You want to carve today's notch on the stick?"

"You'd let me?"

Michael fetched the stick while Christine hid the new lantern under some old hay in the barn.

There were more heat flashes and lightning that night. But if the bolts struck, they hit land already scorched past burning. Daddy, his hands and arms bound worse than Christine's, kept a vigil on the nearby hills, pacing steadily around the perimeter of their buildings, ducking only when a bolt came too close for comfort. Christine stood by the window of her bedroom, counting the minutes it took him to make each revolution, wondering if he'd taken on a sudden death wish, taunting the heavens like that. She finally gave up when Michael called her from the bed.

"What is it?"

"I want to talk about the cave."

She crawled on top of the sheets. "I can't make up any more stories about it. It's too real."

"I'm not sure, Chrissie . . . Sometimes it doesn't seem real at all. Why hasn't anyone else ever found it?"

Christine peeled her hot nightgown from sticky skin. The cloth settled right back down again, clammy. "I thought we'd already decided about that."

"Maybe God did let others find it, others who didn't talk about it, either. Like the Indians."

"Then why haven't we found any people marks in our part of the cave?"

Michael twisted onto an elbow to face her. "There. You said it yourself. *Our* part. Could be other parts, too. Like my crystal room. It could go on forever . . ." He fell onto bony shoulders and stared up to the rough wooden planks of the ceiling. "I sure would like to see where that stream goes. After it disappears into the pond. And all those fish, too. We never did even walk around that pond . . . If we had a boat—"

"If we had a boat, how'd we get it into the cave?

Figure that one out, Michael. And besides, it'd hardly be worthwhile. It seems like such a *small* pond—"

Mama's head poked through the curtain. "Enough whispering, you two. You both need your rest."

"Aw, Mama," grumbled Michael, "not yet."

"Can't sleep with Daddy out there in the night, Ma."

"I can't either, daughter. But the storm's moving off. He should be in soon. Close your eyes."

Christine lay listening to the receding booms, thinking about boats or anything else that might float on water. Strong, wet water.

6

After Christine had finished her morning chores and notched the eighth mark on the stick, she and Michael took to the hills. Their mother watched them go but didn't say anything. She'd been busy concentrating on the plot where the kitchen garden should have been coming up, as if she ought to be on her hands and knees weeding. She seemed not quite sure what to do with herself, bereft of the normal order of things.

Their father had cast off his bandages and was fussing with the truck engine, his head poked under the propped-open hood. Christine knew he was tuning it the best he could, preparing for the leaving. She didn't say as much to Michael, though. Just wondered what California could be like. What any place could be like when you didn't have your roots in it, didn't own a piece of it—and weren't ever likely to without money.

"Look at this, Chrissie!"

Michael was bent over something on the blackened hill to the west of their house.

"What is it?"

He pointed out his find with a smile. "A flower. A flower still blooming. Isn't it amazing? The fire went clear around it."

"It's only a thistle blossom, Michael."

"It's still pretty. And it was saved. Like our place. Find any more on the way back, I'm gonna pick a bunch for Mama."

Inside the big room by the stream, they lay on their backs while Michael gulped lungfuls of air filled with neither smoke nor dust. Christine watched him concentrate on the air, and watched it visibly strengthen him, just as real medicine might work, if they'd had any. He hadn't even paused by the markings to his special room, only headed straight here. Michael knew what he wanted.

The outside of the cave had been a surprise, but Michael hadn't given Christine time to even comment on it, so intent had he been on getting in. The fire had burnt right up to the mouth of the cave, but had skipped the plateau above it. Christine tried to figure it out, but couldn't, so she lay there in the cavern staring at the stone icicles shimmering above her, until her brother finally sat up.

"I'm ready for the rest of the water now, Chrissie."

"What do you mean?"

"I mean it's time to explore around the pond. Find out where it disappears. Just in case it's bigger than we thought."

"I guess it can't hurt. Only don't go getting your hopes up. We still haven't got a boat."

Michael shrugged as if that hardly mattered and picked up his new lantern. Slowly they paced along the stream's edge. The bank didn't ease off gently, like the tiny shore along the Cheyenne River. It was solid rock, solid right up to where the swiftly moving water had cut a channel. Christine suspected it must have taken thousands of years for the stream to carve out the rock that way. And it was still carving, a tiny bit every second.

The room was bigger than either of them had guessed. After they'd reached the pond and walked its known distance, they kept breaking through new blackness, expecting the next steps to bring them up against a solid wall. When it came, Michael bumped right into it.

"Ouch!"

He turned, rubbing his nose. "It seemed like more of the same for sure, Chrissie. My lantern was shining the wrong way."

"You OK?"

"Uh-huh."

But Christine wasn't really paying attention. She was swinging the big kerosene lamp as far as her arm could hold it over the edges of the pond.

"There's an opening in the wall here, Michael. Must be the end of the room. And the pond keeps going right through the arch."

"Let me see!" Michael pushed up next to her. "Water's changing, Chrissie. It's coming together, almost like a river. Look! There's a little stone path on the edge, right through the archway!"

Christine was looking, and seeing. Thinking, too. It was irresistible, but maybe a little tricky . . .

Michael didn't waste time on considerations of any kind. He barreled directly into the arch.

Christine hauled him back. "Where do you think you're going!"

"Hey, watch it! You almost made me slip!"

"Exactly. It's slippery and dangerous in there. Maybe even treacherous—"

"That going to stop you, Chrissie? 'Cause it won't stop me. No, sir. I'd be spending the rest of my life wondering what's through that opening."

Christine loosened her grip on Michael's overalls, but didn't let go completely. "OK. But we've got to be extra careful—"

"You yourself said as how God's watching over us in here, Chrissie!"

"True enough, in a way. He's certainly watching over everything He created in here . . . but I'm not clear on how much leeway He gives for sheer carelessness. I figure you're my lamb, and I'm His stand-in for shepherd. When I say stop, you stop!" Christine eyed her brother. "Is that all definite in your mind, Michael?"

Michael sighed, but managed to calm down some. "Sure, Chrissie. Maybe you better go first."

Christine did go first. Testing each foothold, she stepped into the arch. It spread before them through the dim edges of their lamplight for about fifteen or twenty yards, the quiet pond waters changing each foot of the way. By the end of the arch, it really had turned into a river: a spitting, roiling, frothing mass of waters.

Christine held her lantern before her. Her pace slowed even more as she felt out each step. She was blinded by the close light in the confined space, unsure what would come next. And the sound of all that water kept building in her ears, roaring with ever-greater intensity. She reached out for another step along the ledge, then swiftly drew back her boot to a dead stop. Michael peered over her shoulder, hanging on to her spare arm for safety.

"Wow!"

As Michael's breath was expelled in wonder, Christine's pulled in, till she had a tight, hard knot right under her ribs. The arch over the new river wasn't but a foot or two over their heads. But it wasn't the arch they were staring at.

Through the arch, another chamber opened up. An immense chamber. The river tumbled down into it in a vast cascade of churning waters. They could see it easily, because the roof of the new room before them was lit up and glowing with millions of tiny lights, brighter than the prairie stars on really clear nights.

Christine backed off from the precipice, shaking. Carefully setting down her lamp, she sprawled flat on her chest near the edge, clinging to the solid rock, breathing fast. When she felt she'd made a small contact with something she could understand, something like the coldness and hardness of the rock floor, she inched forward enough to crane her neck again for the view. Wedging himself between his sister and the wall, Michael copied her.

"We'd never get a boat over that, Michael." Christine's voice rose, trying to reach over the great din. "The falls must go down a hundred feet. Maybe more. I can't see the end. Can't even hear it."

"But the lights, Chrissie," Michael shouted back. "What about the lights?"

Christine shook her head. "I don't understand any of it, Michael. But God was really having Himself a good time fixing up this place . . . Maybe it's a kind of joke for what goes on overhead."

Michael was not interested in the theology of the situation. He had a more practical mind. "There's more than enough water here for Daddy. No getting around that."

"True. But it's getting *to* all this water that's the hard part. It feels like we're miles under the earth. Can you imagine snaking pipes in here?" She stopped at a worse thought. "And what would happen if he did, and used it all up? Like those cottonwoods by the Cheyenne?"

"But they were on his land, Chrissie, and he *needed* them."

"Maybe this cave needs the water, too, Michael. Maybe without it all those lights would go out."

Michael studied the magic before him. "Don't know if I could stand for that to happen, Chrissie."

Christine grabbed for her brother's hand. She pressed some warmth into its coldness. "Sinful is what it would be. Worse than cold-blooded murder."

In silent agreement, Michael squeezed back. Then his practicality returned again, banishing thoughts too dire for him to dwell on. "We haven't even started exploring all the walls of our old room, Chrissie. What if there were a tunnel leading from there to the bottom of the falls? Like stairs. We could get in and see it better."

Christine slowly pulled away from the brink, shaking her head. "Not today. We've already been inside here too long. Next thing you know, Daddy will be out hunting after us."

"I'd forgotten about going home, Chrissie."

Christine's head was in a turmoil. "That's not hard to do down here. But we really have to leave. It might take a long time to work back to the string we left by our usual spot."

Michael picked flowers for their mother on the untouched grasses above the cave. Christine helped, noticing for the first time how many there were: mouse ears and prickly pear blooms, and catchflies with their blossoms already closed for the afternoon. She hadn't seen them last time she was up this way with her father, trailing after the elk. She guessed she'd had other things on her mind. Michael pricked a finger on a cactus, but didn't complain. He just sucked at it half the way back.

Mama put the flowers in a little bowl and used them as a centerpiece at the supper table. Baby William leaned out of his high chair and almost toppled everything over, trying to bat at them.

They were eating elk sausage stewed in a jar of Mama's tomato sauce from a kinder summer. Daddy said as how it tasted pretty fair, and Mama took her eyes away from the flowers.

"Why, thank you, Ernest. Making it reminded me of our honeymoon in Hot Springs."

"What's a honeymoon?" Michael wanted to know.

"When a man and a woman get married, dear, they sometimes go off for a little holiday together. If they can afford it." Mama's eyes were far away from the hot kitchen and the half-empty plates. "Your father had a good crop that year, a fine crop . . . My, wouldn't the plunge bath feel good about now."

Daddy was sawing through another sausage. "What brought this on, Clarise?"

"The children bringing me flowers . . . Those meals they served us at the hotel. There were always fresh flowers at table. So refined. And it was the first and last time anybody ever cooked for me. It felt so grand, being treated as if we were just like those rich people come to the spa . . . Don't you remember when they cooked Italian the second night, Ernest?"

Michael wasn't the only one who had his mouth open, with nothing in it. Christine's was agape, too. It seemed like Mama didn't really need the wonders of the cave to cheer her up. A few hill flowers did it just fine.

Daddy stuffed some sausage in his mouth. Mama didn't notice. "They called it spaghetti. Fine, long noodles covered with an herbed tomato sauce. It surely would go well with these sausages."

William got tired of being ignored and made another mighty lunge for the flowers. Christine just managed to catch his chair, narrowly avoiding disaster. Mama forgot about the spaghetti.

It didn't thunder that night. It seemed as if the last batch of lightning had cleaned out the air. Christine had her head and shoulders hanging out the open bedroom window. No dust floating around. Not even any leftover smoke. There were a lot of stars, though. And they were almost as brilliant as the lights in that mysterious cascade room of the cave. She stared at them, wondering. Could there be two parts to the earth—the outside and the inside? Could they be almost opposite to each other, like her cave was to the real world? Which was the real world?

A coyote began to howl from somewhere out there. She stretched farther through the window till she could see it outlined at the top of a hill. He sounded lonely. Or maybe just hungry. Christine hoped that Michael had truly gotten all the chickens put away for the night. She also hoped the coyote found himself a mate.

She pulled herself from the window and edged carefully into the bed. The mattress creaked and sank in the usual places, but Michael slept on. If she ever got married, would her husband take her to Hot Springs on a honeymoon? She fell asleep imagining spaghetti and hot plunge baths and underground stars.

7

When Christine and Michael started sneaking off to the cave the next morning, their father caught them.

"You two've been gallivanting enough lately. And as Michael acts considerable better today, I'll expect some labor from you both."

Christine was hiding the kerosene lamp behind her back, trying not to let the disappointment show. Her father might consider it disrespectful. Lately, he tended to take any haggling over his views, however slight, as disobedience. He didn't used to be like that. He used to enjoy a little give-and-take. The drought had gone and dried all the fun out of him.

"What did you have in mind, Dad?"

"What I had in mind was to start with Big Ben. He needs a proper grooming—"

"You're not really going to sell him, are you, Dad?"

"What?" Michael broke in. "Why in the world would you sell Big Ben, Daddy?"

"I'm *not* going to sell him," their father barked. "Not if I can help it. But I want him looking prime, just in case."

Christine was edging around her father, still attempting to keep the lantern out of sight. "Fair enough. Anything else, Dad?"

"Yes. What's that behind your back?" He spun around to Michael. "You've got something, too. Bring it here, boy, whatever it is."

Michael's face was crinkled, on the verge of breaking out in tears, but he slowly stepped forward to present his cave lamp. They watched their father inspect it.

"You make this, Christine?"

She nodded dumbly.

"It's fair clever. I'd forgotten you had a way with your hands like that. Maybe it's time you started learning about engines." He backed away from Michael and the lard-pail lamp, brushing at his thick hair distractedly. "I'll set you to the tractor's innards after you finish with the mule. The tractor needs to be in order, too."

"Just in case," Christine mumbled to herself, hands

still behind her back. "Sure, Dad," louder. "Be glad to learn about engines." Be glad to do anything to keep you from asking more questions about lamps. In a minute she was inside the barn, getting rid of the evidence. Michael scurried after her.

"He didn't ask what it was for, Chrissie! He didn't ask at all!"

"I know, Michael. I guess Daddy's got other things on his mind these days." She reached for an old bridle hanging on the barn wall. "Here. You'd better fetch Big Ben from the field while I gather grooming supplies. It might take a few minutes to find them. Big Ben hasn't had a proper brushdown since I can remember."

Big Ben stood stolidly in the shade of the barn under the *Orange Crush* sign while they worked him over. Christine trimmed his hooves while Michael, perched on an old wood-slatted apple crate, concentrated on getting tangles from his stiff, short mane. Loose patches were clipped from his side, and Christine even gave a shot at cleaning his teeth with a short-handled brush. At that, the mule brayed out his displeasure and gave Michael a sideways kick, knocking him off the box.

"Hey! No fair! It's not me that's poking in your mouth, Big Ben. Why don't you go for Chrissie?" Michael rubbed at his hip. "Gonna be black-and-blue all over."

"Pipe down, Michael, he didn't kick you that hard." Christine grasped open the mule's lips again. "Ugh. His choppers are nasty, for sure. All stained brown. You ought to be taking better care of your teeth, Big Ben. If they go, so do you."

Big Ben snapped.

She whipped her fingers out of biting range. "All right, then, if that's how you feel about it . . . I don't know, Michael. It's pretty hard to make a silk purse out of a sow's belly. Any way you look at it, Big Ben's a fairly old mule. I can't see anybody paying good money for him."

Michael was rubbing the animal's long ears, his hurt already forgotten. "Why's Daddy want to sell him? When the rain comes, we'll be needing Big Ben. Won't we, boy," he crooned into the mule's ears. "You'll feel much better getting all messy again, plowing through the fields."

Christine glanced up into the clear sky, devoid of any cloud whatsoever. "When the rain comes."

Michael saddle-soaped the ancient, cracked harness in the afternoon. He didn't work too hard at it. He was acting tired again. Every so often, Christine glanced over from where she was fussing with bits and pieces her father had pulled out of the tractor engine, carefully polishing and greasing each, trying to get rid of clinging dust.

"Why don't you take a nap, Michael?" she said eventually.

"I don't want to go in the house. Mama would fuss.

Besides, William's already had his nap and he'd climb all over me, wanting attention."

"Crawl into the loft, away from the hay. Daddy's got a pile of clean canvas up there. I won't make any noise."

Michael hesitated over his chore, but finally got up. "This doesn't mean I won't be strong enough for the cave tomorrow, Chrissie."

"I know, Michael. It's all right."

Christine had most of the tractor's engine parts laid out, gleaming, when Mama called them in for supper. She woke Michael and they both stopped by the water pump on the way in. Christine washed off engine grime, Michael the telltale signs of sleep.

Mama had the soup bowls out and was already ladling broth into them.

"Where'd you get the soup, Ma?"

"Your father brought me a chicken. He said it was molting anyway, so we might as well make use of it."

Christine stared at the soup her mother placed before her. It had little dumplings floating in it and smelled good. The chicken meat for afters would be a treat, too, just like a proper Sunday dinner back in the old days. But it was just one more sign. Only twelve days until Daddy planned to leave. And the chickens couldn't come with them.

Christine overheard her parents talking again that night. This time she was eavesdropping in earnest, sitting up next to Michael's curled body, her head forward, hair shoved behind her ears.

"The Finleys are moving out to California, Clarise. In another week or so."

"What will happen to their land?"

"I guess they'll just abandon it. There's nobody around to buy it. Not even the bank still open in Rapid City."

Christine heard her mother shoving around a cup on the kitchen table. They must be having coffee.

"What will they do in California? Oh, Ernest, what will *we* do in California?"

"I'm strong. I'm a good farmer—given a little water. I've read about it in the newspapers in town. Orange groves they've got, and grapes. Even something called 'avocados' they're trying out. We could follow the crops."

"All of us? Like gypsies? Without a home of our own? . . . And you've always been independent. You've never worked for another man, Ernest."

He ignored the part about gypsies. "I guess it's time I was learning."

Christine heard him push back his chair. Heard him pour from the coffeepot.

"I thought I'd drive into town tomorrow. At least make an effort at finding a buyer for some of our things."

"Are you truly set on this, Ernest? Isn't there any

other way for us to stay? Maybe you should have taken over my father's store when he offered it to you, before he died. Maybe you could have kept it from going bankrupt—"

"You know I can't be cooped up like that, Clarise. I never could. Working the land is all I ever wanted. Working my *own* land." He stopped. "I guess working somebody else's land will just have to be second best."

Christine waited for her mother's answer. It wasn't exactly accepting, more wistful. "Please take me along, then, tomorrow. I'd like to visit with my parents at the cemetery. Maybe for the last time."

"What about the children?"

"I'll take the baby. Christine and Michael have sense enough to look after themselves."

Christine sank back into the mattress and pulled a sheet over her head. It was all happening too fast.

In the morning, their father laid out chores for Christine and Michael before hustling Mama and the baby into the pickup and pulling out. Christine watched the truck snake through their land and over the next hill, plumes of dust following it.

Then she turned to Michael. "Go get the lanterns."

"But Daddy said—"

"Get the lanterns. The chores will keep. The cave may not."

"What do you mean?"

But Christine was already striding west into the hills.

Once down the long passageway, Christine did not head for the stream. Instead, she angled off to the right, systematically inspecting the chamber's walls foot by foot, her lantern beam becoming an aggressive searchlight.

The first tunnel they found led to a room crammed with brownish-red latticework. It was different from anything they'd seen so far—not nearly as fragile and showy as the crystals in Michael's room. It was more workmanlike, as if a sturdy brick wall had been built, then carefully removed, leaving only the mortar. In point of fact, it was a lot similar to that closed-down brick bank in town, still standing, without the support of its money.

"Say, this stuff is interesting, Chrissie."

"It is, but we're moving on." She grabbed at Michael.

He batted off her hand. "What's the big hurry, anyway? We didn't stop for the stream or the fish, and you practically shoved me down this tunnel—"

"We need to find the staircase to the cascade room."

"Sure, but—"

"Don't argue, Michael. Just follow me."

The second tunnel led to a dead end, the third to a gaping crack in the floor that Christine, in her headlong rush, half plunged into. She floundered from the edge, both legs dangling into the void.

"Help! Grab the lantern, Michael . . . Grab me!"

He dropped his own light to catch the lantern, to reach for an arm, hanging on with all his strength till she'd regained a toehold and laboriously scrambled to safety.

Michael flopped down, huffing for breath, eyeing his sister. "You said we had to be careful in the cave, Chrissie. And here you go, nearly killing yourself. You're not making any sense." He swallowed more air. "Also, you're wearing me out."

"I did *not* nearly kill myself. I merely tripped in a little hole—"

"Little hole, my foot! Big enough to swallow both of us, that hole is."

"Come and see who's right, Mr. Know-It-All."

Michael inched over on his knees and they both shone their lanterns into the gap.

"Boy." Michael whistled. "Does that ever go down a long way." His whistle returned to him, amplified. He whistled some more.

Christine was feeling a little green in her stomach area. A trifle light-headed, too. If she'd been barreling through here without her brother . . .

"Stop the noise, Michael. I'm trying to hear if there are any water sounds down there."

Michael unpursed his lips and cocked an ear. Then he picked up a loose pebble and tossed it down the opening. It clattered off the sides for a long time before they heard a final, faint *ping*.

"It hit bottom. No water there, Chrissie. But it sure

is a fair ways down. Far enough down to break every bone in your body, and then some."

"Not *my* body. A *person's* body."

"It was *your* body dangling into it, not some other person's body."

"All right already. Thank you for helping me." Christine caught her grudging tone but didn't try to correct it. She didn't care for being proven dead wrong. She stared into the abyss a final time before moving from the edge. "We couldn't explore it without a good rope anyhow. A longer piece of rope than Daddy owns. Let's go."

Despite her close call, Christine still ventured through the dark shadows of the fourth tunnel with determination. It began to lull them into hope for success as it plunged steadily toward the center of the earth at a firm angle of descent. It went on so far that they ran out of string and yarn both. Only then did she call a halt.

"We can't go any farther, Michael. It wouldn't be safe."

"Glad to see you putting some thought into safety all of a sudden. But it's all right with me." Michael was puffing for breath. "I'm clean wore out with all this rushing, anyways. It's more fun when we take our time. You're making it like work today, Chrissie."

Christine knew she'd been pushing relentlessly, but she also knew the reason. Michael didn't. She also knew she wasn't being fair to him, but couldn't do anything about that, either. On top of which she'd lost all track of time.

"We'd better climb back to the stream and rest up a little. You'll need your strength to get home."

When they did return, trouble was waiting. Daddy and Mama and baby William had gotten home earlier than expected, to no children and undone chores. Christine spotted the truck first. Next she saw her father standing by the house, his eyes searching the hills. She looked up into the sky. Maybe their parents hadn't gotten home as soon as all that. Worked up like she was, she hadn't even noticed the sun setting behind them from the west.

Michael stated the obvious. "We're in for it now."

"Drop your lantern. Daddy would ask about it this time for sure."

Empty-handed, they went down the hill to get their just rewards.

_____

Their father was still steaming fifteen minutes later. He'd begun simmering in the yard, then had hauled them into the kitchen to really boil. Christine hadn't realized he owned such a temper, or so many words.

And he hadn't let them insert so much as a syllable. Not that Christine had invented a reasonable excuse yet, at least nothing she wanted to use as an excuse. The cave was out, that was sure. She didn't want to get into the leaving business, either. Michael shouldn't have to know about that. Between the cave and the hope for rain, he'd changed a lot in the past few weeks, becoming stronger—and more sure-minded, too. Take away the mystery and the hope and what would he have left to work for?

". . . never knew I'd raised two such thoughtless, inconsiderate children . . ."

Christine began to tune back in again. Her father's voice seemed to go up and down, in and out, just like songs she'd heard on the radio at the general store in town. Only Daddy wasn't making music.

". . . no sense of responsibility, leaving the chickens to peck at their eggs, and your mother and I to worry ourselves silly . . ."

Baby William was howling, obviously just as upset as Daddy over the whole business. Michael was working a boot toe into the hard wood of the kitchen floor. His head down, he pushed at that one spot over and over again, as if he was aiming to dig clear through to the root cellar beneath.

". . . it's got to stop, and it *will* stop!"

Christine glanced up. Had her father run out of breath? He was removing his handkerchief from a pocket and wiping at his neck. In the background, Mama's stove noises were suddenly very loud. Christine cleared her throat.

"Sorry to disappoint you so, Daddy. Michael and I, we just lost track of time. It won't happen again—even if these walks in the hills seem to help Michael's breathing like they do."

Mama spoke for the first time. "It's a wonder, but she's right about that, Ernest."

Their father glared, his face red clear through its deep tan. "You're not to go off these premises one single day for the next week. Either of you. Is that understood?"

Christine gulped. An entire week out of the eleven days left didn't give them anywhere near enough time. "Couldn't we make it just three days, Dad? We'll work like the dickens—"

"No!"

Daddy stormed out of the shack, slamming the screen door.

Christine started setting the table, avoiding her mother's anxious glance. One single *day*. He'd said that right out. Hadn't said a thing about *nights*, though.

A cave didn't care about the time of day. It didn't care about time at all. No clocks in there, ticking away. No sun rising up and setting down. Nothing but endlessness, marked by a few drips of water.

Three nights later, honorably keeping to her own measure of the punishment deserved, Christine eased Michael out the bedroom window after their parents were long asleep. Shoving out her own feet, she landed beside him, motioning for complete silence. Boots slung around their necks, they tiptoed across the hardscrabble yard till they reached the relative softness of the first dried grass. They didn't linger there, though, but climbed the hill to the spot where they'd dropped their lanterns. Both were still waiting.

"Got enough kerosene, Chrissie?" Michael wondered as he laced up his boots.

"I snuck out and filled it up this morning," she answered. "Got two fresh candles, too."

"Should we light them now?"

"No. The moon's bright enough to see by. We don't want to waste them."

They walked along awhile in silence.

"Lucky you made me take another nap in the barn this afternoon, Chrissie."

"I know. We're going to have to be real careful tonight. We can't stay overlong. Can't lose track of the time. Only an hour or so, that's all we've got."

"You have the extra string?"

Christine patted a bulge in her dress pocket. "I had to unravel that old sweater of mine, the green one that was getting too small anyway."

"I thought that was supposed to be mine next."

"It was. Maybe it still could be. We finish the exploring, I'll have Ma teach me how to knit. She's been wanting to, anyway, for the longest time."

"How come you didn't let her?"

"I didn't have a good enough reason. Knitting's got to be the most boring job possible without a good reason."

"Shivering to death in the winter sounds like a good enough reason to me."

"It's barely June, Michael. We'll cross that bridge when we come to it."

The hole in the hill gaped blacker than usual as they paused to fumble with matches. A sudden cloud out of nowhere covered the moon's face and a distant coyote set up a mournful cry. Christine's hand trembled unaccountably. Finally, the flame caught the kerosene and the lamp's warm glow enveloped them. Easing into the cave was simple after that, and once they were inside, its familiar sensation wrapped itself around them.

"Makes me feel as if I'm inside a cocoon sometimes," Christine murmured. "Safe, my wings ready to fly any moment I choose."

"It makes *me* feel like I'm wrapped in a hug from Mama . . . Haven't been all that many hugs from her lately, though. Think she's using them all up on baby William?"

Christine started through the passageway, her lantern a beacon to the beyond. "Somehow I don't think that's it at all, Michael. If I were a mother, seems like there'd always be hugs to spare. They don't cost a thing, do they? . . . Nope," she answered for herself, "don't cost a thing. But maybe you've got to be in the right frame of mind."

"Mama sure was when I handed her those flowers. Thought she'd squeeze me to death on the spot."

"Mama's just not been getting enough flowers lately.

We'll have to keep that in mind, and maybe try to fix the situation."

The sound of the stream reached them, and soon they were in their big room. Instead of going right, along the wall to the tunnel they needed to finish exploring, Christine led on to the stream's edge, to their usual resting and thinking spot.

"I thought you were in a big hurry again, Chrissie."

Christine was kneeling by the edge, fluttering fingers in the water in search of playful fish. She laughed as one brushed her, then seemed to come back to rub her palm.

"Look, Michael! This fish is swimming right in place by my hand. I really think it wants to be petted and scratched, like Big Ben."

Michael leaned over to admire the ten-inch fish. "It's smaller than the others. Think it's a baby?" His hand plunged in. "Where's behind a fish's ears, Chrissie? Big Ben sheer enjoys scratches behind the ears."

"Guess at it, Michael. This fish likes to be patted down its side, too. It's wiggling with happiness!"

The creature kept dancing within their caresses until it finally rolled over and over and abandoned itself, almost regretfully, to the currents. Christine drank from the stream where it had been.

"What we did wrong last time, Michael . . . what *I* did wrong: it finally came to me."

Michael neatly cupped his hand for his own drink.

"Didn't know we'd done anything wrong. We didn't make that big crack in the tunnel. I don't like to rush like that, is all."

"You understood, but didn't know why. Now I know. We tried to get something out of the cave, instead of enjoying it. We started to take its wonders for granted."

Michael slurped some more, cogitating. "Are you trying to tell me we can't go on exploring?"

"Of course not! If God made all this for us, I expect He wants us to find everything by and by. But in good time, not greedily. Not so we dash past the small wonders for the bigger ones. I truly do believe He loves each and every tiny crystal as much as that whole cascade room. Just like Mama loves each and every one of us at home."

Michael jumped to his feet and brushed at his overall knees. "Glad you got that all sorted out to your satisfaction, Chrissie, 'cause I think it means we can hunt for the staircase again."

Christine groaned. "Don't boys ever hear anything but what they want to hear?"

"There's nothing wrong with my ears." Michael grinned. "Nothing wrong with any part of me down here when you aren't rushing me. But if you expect to get home before that old rooster crows—"

Christine slapped her forehead. "The time! Only that one tunnel, Michael." Her head craned toward the ceiling arching out of sight above her. "And if we seem to be rushing, Lord, don't hold it against us. Don't hold anything against our Daddy, either. He just can't see beyond his need for rain." She picked up her lantern and shifted her face up again. "But a little water on the outside wouldn't come amiss, Lord. It truly wouldn't." She added an "Amen" as Michael dragged her off.

The extra yarn got them to the end of the fourth tunnel. It didn't finish up by the falling river, but in a perfect circular room with its own kind of water.

His lamp shifting with his head, Michael peered around curiously. "It seems like part of our river got frozen in here, Chrissie. Into little waterfalls."

Her own lamplight showed her it was true. Perfect columns of water, stilled for eternity, graced the wall at almost equal intervals. Some columns were white, some golden, some pink as the dawn sky in the east. Christine touched one. "It's cool and hard, not even damp."

Michael was running a finger over another pillar. "And so shiny! Almost as if somebody's been down here polishing at it." He tiptoed to the center of the room to take in the entire circle at once. When he tripped on a loose rock, he looked down.

"Chrissie!"

"What is it?" She was already going to him, afraid to move too quickly, afraid their coming would change something, as it had in Michael's Room. But this room was made of firmer stuff. Nothing tinkled, nothing moved. She lowered her lantern next to her brother's. Then she saw.

"*Fish*, Michael! Fish the same as in the water, frozen forever."

Her brother was touching the images. "Look at this one. It's the same size as the fish that was playing with us by the stream. And it's got that funny kind of blind eye, too. Only it's hard rock."

"Feel the scales, every one of them perfect. And this next one's got all its bones showing!" Christine's eyes hovered, moving at last to swim past the fish, over the mosaic of the floor. "More fish, different kinds. And smaller creatures. Are they bugs?"

"No kind of bugs I've ever seen, Chrissie."

"Of course not. This is the inside world. It would have different kinds of bugs than the outside world. The same as how it's got different kinds of fish."

"Could be a time it was all the same world, couldn't it?"

"Not for a million, billion years, Michael."

Michael started to argue about that estimation, but Christine stopped listening. Inside her head she heard another voice. Strange. Sounded like a cock crowing, loud and clear. She jumped up.

"It's late, Michael. Way late!"

They dashed back along the path of their yarn, Christine balling it up as fast as she could with one hand also jiggling the lantern. They burst into the big room and practically ran along its wall to the passageway out. Beneath the hole to the upper world, Christine sighed a huge sigh of relief. It was still night-black outside.

She boosted Michael up the rope with fervor. Together, they hustled from the cave's mouth, speeding over the hills to drop their lanterns in the same spot they'd abandoned them earlier, only a bald hummock away from the steep slope of their home gully.

Below, their house was quiet. Nothing stirred. As they crept in the rear window and into bed, the rooster crowed for sure, loud and vigorous. Christine pulled the sheets over their clothes and dropped straight into sleep.

Mama had to shake hard to wake her.

"Christine. Christine, honey. You've slept clean through breakfast, and your father's waiting for you outside."

Christine creaked open an eye. It was an effort, like shoving at the barn door in the winter when it was caked with ice. "It can't be morning already, Ma. I only got to sleep."

Her mother bent to grace her with a rare kiss. Then she felt for her brow. "You're not sick, are you, dear? I know things haven't been easy lately, but I couldn't stand it if you went and got sick. I *rely* on you, daughter."

Christine struggled up. "I'm not sick, Ma, just tired—"

"Goodness, gracious! You slept in your clothes all night? And a sweater, too? There must be a summer influenza I haven't heard about!" She stopped. "Or worse, the malarial ague."

"Mosquitoes haven't been that bad yet. I just felt cold last night, Ma. Nothing to get excited over." Christine pulled herself from the bed, careful to keep the sheet high around Michael. Having Ma see him in his overalls wouldn't simplify matters. "Let Michael sleep a little longer. I'll feed the chickens for him."

A little wobbly on both legs, Christine tried a bright smile for her mother. "See, I saved a bunch of time, not having to get dressed all over again. Now I can run out to the chores direct."

Mama shook her head, a gesture of half exasperation, half concern. "Not until you've tucked some food into your stomach. When you're walking a straight line, we'll see about the chores."

Christine staggered through the curtain after her mother. The cave might not know the difference between night and day, but her body surely did. And it wasn't at all pleased by the confusion in the proper order of things.

"About time" was all her father said when Christine finally made it to the yard.

"You had something special in mind, Dad?" She watched his boots raise small puffs of dust as he clumped past her.

"I need another set of hands for the back of the pickup."

Christine turned to the truck and blinked. Something was different about it. If she'd been as clearheaded as usual, it ought to be obvious. That was it. He'd gone and set uprights into all four corners of the bed. "Isn't that some of your irrigation pipe, Dad?"

"You're waking up. I need you to hold the cross-pieces for the top."

Christine clambered up the back of the truck, scuffing a knee in the process. "Maybe it's 'cause I'm not *entirely* woke up yet, but what you fixing to do with all these pipes?"

"Here."

He handed her the first long crosspiece. It was heavy. Christine juggled it uncomfortably, arms stretched, until she had one end astride the top of a corner pipe. Her father jumped onto the dented fender to work with the wire in his hand. The fender sagged. He slid down and climbed into the rear of the truck bed to try again.

"My grandfather came to these parts in a covered wagon. It's fitting we leave the same way."

Christine's throat was suddenly dry. She swallowed to try to moisten it, but it didn't help. Daddy was talking outright about *leaving*. Not to Mama, to *her*. "What do you mean, Dad?"

He shot her a look. "May have raised you partways irresponsible, but I never did raise you dumb. You *know* what I mean. The rains haven't come."

"But you yourself said we had three weeks. When we went after the elk—"

"Hold that pipe steady. I can't work with you shaking it that way."

Christine summoned fresh iron into her arms. The pipe steadied. "Three weeks, Dad. Your very words. And there's an entire week left."

"How do you know?"

"Like you said, I'm not dumb. I've been keeping track."

"Balance the end of that pipe over to the other upright."

Christine did her father's bidding. He moved down the truck bed to continue his fussing.

"We can't leave before the last week is out."

"Who says, daughter?"

"It would be giving in. It wouldn't be fighting the battle proper."

"Didn't know we were in a war here," her father mumbled.

"What else you want to call it, Daddy? We've been fighting the wind and the dust and the heat seems like forever. We oughtn't give up now, when it's so close."

"What's so close?"

"Why, the rain!"

Her father dropped his spool of wire and stared at her. "How do you come to be so certain? You know something I don't? You have a telegraph line hooked up with the Almighty?"

Christine pulled back into herself, shaking her head. It was too much to explain. Already she'd let the cave business and what it signified to her go past explaining, even if she'd wanted to. She'd never find the proper words for it, anyway.

"I'll help you get ready. Just promise me we won't leave till the next seven days are past."

Daddy yanked at the newly wired pipe with choler. He yanked so hard the whole contraption fell apart, the pipe bouncing onto his boots. "*You'll* help me, Miss Princess? Out of the bounty of your heart, I suppose? Who, just *who* are you to be giving orders to your father? Twelve years old and you have all the answers?"

Christine backed away and was about to jump off the truck bed, but her father had the pipe lifted up again.

"Get back here! I still need your hands. But not your mouth."

Christine shut up.

Her father didn't talk to her the rest of that blessed day. But he didn't let her go, either. He pointed, or nodded his head, or grunted. Christine always jumped fast.

Michael waltzed out just before lunchtime, assessed the situation, and ran for the neglected chickens. Daddy didn't even go into the house for his meal. Michael had to deliver fried elk-sausage sandwiches and the water pail for the two of them. Long hours later, when Mama yelled that supper was ready, the truck was just about finished.

Christine chanced a look at her father and he muttered something. Taking that to mean she was excused at last, she jumped off the truck. They'd finally gotten all the crossbars in place and strengthened. Next they'd slung up every piece of spare canvas sitting around the barn loft. So much for Michael's nap place. Now the canvas billowed softly in the usual evening wind, lashed down from the outside with rope. If you were to ignore the rubber tires holding up the truck bed, and the engine in the front where oxen ought to be, the whole thing did look like a covered wagon.

Christine scratched at her head absentmindedly. The pioneers might have had an edge on her family, though. Oxen ate grass. Even dry, stunted grass was free. The truck ate gasoline, and that wasn't. They couldn't be shoving their everlasting supply of elk sausage into it, either. What happened when the gas tank went dry? They might end up stranded someplace more desolate than their own piece of burnt, rainless prairie. Had her father thought about all this? Had he worked out eventualities?

Even if they made it to California, a covered wagon wouldn't make any kind of a home. The guaranteed land out there had been used up by gold seekers— that's what her teacher had called them—almost a hundred years ago. And if it was all orange groves and strange things like avocados now, there wouldn't be elk to hunt, either. Christine jumped and spun as someone touched her shoulder.

"What do *you* want, Michael?"

"Why're you shouting at me, Chrissie? What did I do? Mama only wants to know did you hear her call for supper. It's getting cold setting out at table."

"I'm coming."

But she didn't. She stood inspecting the truck some more. Michael stood beside her. Christine finally noticed that tears had started down his cheeks.

"For heaven's sake, I didn't yell at you that badly. What's the matter?"

"I only now figured it out. Daddy's gonna make us go away, isn't he? He's gonna put all our things inside that truck and just drive away."

Christine put her arm around her brother's shoulder. "Maybe."

Michael jerked away, the tears still streaming. "Don't treat me like a baby anymore, Chrissie. I'm grown enough to know that when Daddy makes up his mind the rest of us—not even Mama—don't count for beans." He swiped at his face with his bare arm. "We have to do what Daddy says."

"Maybe the new place—California—won't have any dust, Michael. You could breathe proper all the time."

Michael's eyes turned dry and hard. "It for sure won't have a cave, Chrissie."

9

Mama's dried-out supper had been eaten in glum silence by all. When they finally crawled into bed, Christine turned full away from her brother, wanting total privacy to fume. She hadn't ever felt exactly this way before. Hadn't ever felt the need for her own bed, her own room, just her own self. Michael had always been a comfort, a small warm body to snuggle up to, even when he was feeling poorly. When Michael tapped her shoulder, she growled, just like Daddy. He tapped again, more insistently.

"What about the cave, then?"

"I don't want to talk about the cave, Michael. Don't want to talk about anything. Let me be."

"And the rain. What about the rain? If we were to take off tomorrow, what if it rained the next day?"

"It won't rain. It's never going to rain again in our lifetimes. Not on this land. Not anywhere in South Dakota."

"That's not so, Chrissie, and you know it. There's still six and a half entire days left. I had to make the mark on the stick today. You were too busy."

"Don't care about the silly stick anymore," muttered Christine, clamping the pillow over her head.

Michael dragged it loose. "*I* care about the stick. It's not silly. And I care about the cave, too. I want to go back there. Tonight."

"Not on your life." Christine wrestled the pillow from his hands and pulled it over her head again, this time anchoring it firmly with her fingers.

Patiently, Michael pried each of her tensed fingers free and levered the pillow up. "Why? You gonna give up like Daddy? You going to get into that ratty old Ford and just drive off forever and never go back to the cave again? You're never even going to think about the cave again? Tell me that, Chrissie. Tell me you can do that."

Christine turned and glared at her brother. "I can do that."

"Liar! You're lying, and I never knowed you to do that before. And never to me."

"I lied lots of times, Michael. All those stories I made up. Lies, all of them."

"Stories aren't lies. Stories are stories. They make you dream nice things, like the cave does. And the cave isn't a lie."

Christine sat up, hair askew, nightgown in a jumble. "Maybe we needed it so badly we both made it up. Maybe we've been walking in a dream, living in a dream, the whole time we're there."

Michael was up now, too, on his knees in front of her. "Prove it!" he spat out. "Prove the whole thing isn't real!"

Christine ran her hands through her stringy hair. She sighed. "You win. We'll go."

Baby William had been mostly sleeping through the night lately, but just in case he yelled for their mother, Christine forced Michael to help her stuff their extra set of clothing and the winter quilts under the sheet. Christine patted them into appropriate-sized body lumps until she was satisfied. When she finished, Michael had already slithered out the window.

They climbed in mutually defiant silence to the lamps. Sullenly they pulled on boots and paced the hills. Christine only let up once. It was to yelp when she bumped her shin against the sharp needles of a prickly pear. Michael stopped, but didn't offer either solace or a hand. He merely stood waiting until she'd pulled the obvious needles from her bare leg and cast an accusing stare where the moon should have been in the sky. It'd been nearly full last night. Why wasn't it doing its job now? Only dark blankness met her eyes.

Even the mouth of the cave wasn't the same. To-night, when they needed the solace of the usual refresh-ing, cool breeze worse than ever, the hole nearly sucked them into itself. Christine half tumbled down the rope, almost inhaled by the strength of it. She shielded the madly flickering flame of the lantern to her chest as Michael fell atop her.

"What's happening, Chrissie?" He struggled up, bracing his body from the wind, forgetting his anger.

"I'm not sure. I don't know . . ." Her voice was dragged out of her. "But I'll bet we get to the big room in record time."

It felt as if they were being tossed through the center of a threshing machine as the winds buffeted them through the long passageway. Michael clung to his homemade lamp grimly, never even thinking to relight it once its flame had been extinguished. Where the pas-sageway hurled them into the large chamber, the wind died.

Christine lurched to the nearest wall, clinging to the roughness until her legs became strong again. "I think I need the water, Michael."

He nodded his understanding and followed.

"Does the stream seem stronger to you, Michael?" They were sitting, staring into the narrow currents.

"Could be. It's got a feisty kind of look to it tonight. Aren't any fish jumping around, either."

"I noticed."

They stared some more.

"How are we gonna get back out, Chrissie? I never felt a wind that strong before. I've still got goose bumps from it." He rubbed at his arms, frowning.

"I don't know, Michael. I really don't know."

Michael began studying the big room, as if he were seeing it for the first time. "It is real. All of it. Nobody could make it up just out of their head. Not even the world's greatest liar."

She nodded. There wasn't anything she could say. She'd always known it was real. Down here, it was easy to believe. It was harder outside. It was hard to believe anything outside with Daddy falling to pieces the way he was. And the truck turned into a covered wagon . . . and the family about to become rootless wanderers.

"We might never find the secret staircase now, Chrissie."

"I know that, too."

"Could we look at the magical room again? Just once more? I'd hate to leave without seeing it once more."

"Sure. Why not." Christine pushed herself up. Might as well have a little happiness before they destroyed themselves trying to get back home through that wind in the passageway.

Christine relit Michael's candle and they walked along the stream. It became more agitated at its merging into the pond. And the pond itself had changed. Its usual placid surface was now furrowed with small waves. They neared the archway where it disappeared. The water level had risen, almost lapping over the top of their pathway ledge. But not quite. Christine decided they could chance it, that they needed to chance it. She took the first step.

The burgeoning river spit at them each foot of the way. They were drenched to the bone in cold water when they finally clung, heedless, to the far edge. The sight was worth it.

The river still tumbled endlessly over the brink, and the vast ceiling beyond still glowed. But something was different. Bits of the stars were floating between the cataract and the nothingness. Twinkling, fluttering, swooping, they descended, defining momentary spaces in the void.

Christine and Michael lay there for a long time, watching. Nothing changed yet everything was new. Finally Christine noticed the cold. She pulled Michael away and they retraced their steps back to safety. There they stood, outside the arch, dripping, smiling.

"Even if we never come back, that makes it all worth it, Chrissie."

"Yes. It does." She began to wring out her skirt.

Michael stooped to do the same with his overall legs, then hesitated. Still bent, he picked up something. "If we were to have more weight, might be we could fight that wind in the passage."

"How do you mean?"

"It bashed me around considerable on the way in. It's gonna be worse going out, too, against the force. I was thinking if I were big as Daddy, it couldn't treat me that way." He showed her what he'd found. It was an oblong stone, rounded smoothly on all sides, just big enough to fill an overall pocket. "If we tuck a few of these in our clothes, they could give us some of that weight."

"You know I don't want to take anything out of the cave, Michael!"

"Not even us?"

Christine bent to find some stones.

They were so laden they were already staggering under their burdens by the time they neared the exit passageway. Christine was beginning to consider the whole business totally ridiculous. They'd overestimated the force of that wind. Just gone and let their imaginations play with them again.

Until she bent into the tunnel. In a split second she was spewed out again, right onto her bottom. She turned to frown automatically at Michael's chuckle. But he wasn't laughing. He was scared silly, his teeth chattering loud enough to hear.

"All right, then, Michael. We're going to have to do this together. You lock your arm into mine and don't let go for anything. Understand?"

His head went up and down. He was too frightened to talk.

"Do it now! We can't wait here all night!"

Michael finally managed a few words. "Why . . . why not?"

Even with all those rocks tucked into all his overall pockets, he was chickening out.

"Because we don't know how long the wind will last. It's gone the other way, gently, for days. Could be it's decided to turn itself around for another few weeks."

It was hard, making herself sound like she knew what she was doing. Like an authority. Like her father. But in certain situations somebody had to be in charge. Maybe it was hard for Daddy, too. That was her last conscious thought as Michael latched on and Christine stepped into the tunnel.

Michael's candle was blown out instantly. Christine's lamp lasted another few seconds. When it went, the nightmare of the wind became worse. They stumbled and clawed against it as against a monster reaching out for them, trying to crush them in its colossal grip. Each step forward seemed to take them five back. There was no way of knowing, of assessing their progress. They were completely blind. Horrifyingly blind.

Christine's head churned from the steady howling in her ears, her very brain. Even the sound of the wind was a cutting agony. They could be pulled into one of the side tunnels and lost forever. Who knew the ways of this wind?

In a moment of clarity, she realized who knew.

Lord, she prayed inside her pounding head. *Lord. You made the cave and the wind. Get us out. Please.*

Christine banged into a hard wall, tripped, dropped her lantern, and groped for it, for anything. Michael, clinging like bottom-of-the-bucket molasses, fell with her. Her hand still reaching, groping, felt something. It was the string. The string to the entrance! On all fours she pulled at it, as if it would drag them to the entrance of its own accord. That's when she noticed something else. The wind wasn't as strong next to the floor of the passageway. She tried to say something to Michael, but couldn't. He'd noticed, anyway. Heads down, fingering the string respectfully, prayerfully, they crawled forward.

Out of the mouth, away from the wind, they lay on the burned grass, their chests heaving. Christine finally noticed that it was still night. The shapes of the hills around them slowly took on definition. She could see again. The blindness had passed.

"We lost the lanterns, Chrissie."

"It doesn't matter. We can find them again when the wind changes."

"I'm never going back inside until it does."

"Nobody's going to make you, Michael."

"Good."

Christine felt her dress and sweater. She'd been sopping wet from the river. Now her clothing was bone-dry. Her hair, too. It wasn't nearly light enough to see properly by, but she touched her skirt again, for comfort. It was in shreds. Her legs were stinging, too. She reached down a hand and it came away stained and damp in the darkness. It wasn't just the cactus needles. She'd been skinned within an inch of her life by that flight through the tunnel. Slowly she got to her feet. Everything ached. Every bone and muscle in her body. She reached out a hand to Michael.

"Can you make it back? We might have to do some explaining this time. In the morning."

He shook cave stones loose from his pockets. "Explaining to Daddy and Mama can't be worse than what we just been through."

Christine boosted Michael through the window first. When she followed, she had a surprise. Mama was sitting on the edge of their bed in the dark, nursing baby William. It took a while to work out all the familiar shapes in the dark, too long to sneak out the window again. Besides, Christine had no desire to be back in the night. She was utterly weary and only wanted her bed.

Michael stood stock-still in front of their mother. Christine kept a step behind him. Their mother said nothing, but when a tear ran down her face to fall on William's head, Christine heard it plop. William burped and Mama creaked up to nestle him in his crib.

Only then did she turn to her two others, whispering. "Your daddy doesn't need this heartache on top of everything else. In the morning we'll talk."

Christine badly wanted to reach out for her mother and hug her, badly wanted to tell her everything was all right. But it wasn't really all right, was it? Maybe nothing would ever be all right again. Her mother disappeared through the curtain, yet Michael still stood there, frozen. Gently, Christine propelled him into bed. When she followed him, he was shivering all over. She held his hand until his muscles slowly began to relax.

10

Morning never seemed to come. Christine wasn't sure whether she slept or dreamed or just worried. If she dreamed, it was a nightmare. Winds roiled about her, tossing her into walls and ceilings at first, next into rocks and up against rough hills. When she opened her eyes, she was stiff and clammy all over from the beating and Michael next to her had begun to shiver again. Maybe he'd never stopped. She reached a hand to his face. It was burning hot and wet. The wind and the tunnel had been too much. She'd gone and got him sick again, after all the weeks of struggle.

Christine shifted her body to raise her eyes to the

window. Surely it must be past daybreak. Yet the sky was as gray and roiled as her dreams. She trembled helplessly and reached for one of the winter quilts that'd gotten shoved down by her feet. She pulled it up around her and Michael. It wasn't her imagination. They were both shivering, true, but so was the house. There was a cold wind, a winter wind, blowing through the open window and the slats.

When baby William woke up with a yelp of confusion, Christine finally hauled herself from under the covers and shut the window. Where was her mother?

Christine carried the baby out to the kitchen and sat him in his high chair. William was hungry and both her parents were gone. That was good and bad. She knew she had to face up to her mother sometime, but she wasn't anywhere near ready yet. Truth to tell, she might never be ready. She'd waited too long. How to explain that she'd only wanted something of her very own?

She should have told Mama about the cave right after that business with the flowers, when Ma was in the right frame of mind. How could anything Christine had to say now make up for the hurt in her mother last night? Anger was way easier to deal with than hurt any day.

She checked the stove. Warm oatmeal sat there. Wordlessly, Christine filled a bowl and began to feed William. He chomped into it greedily, so greedily that when the spoon missed he went for her finger and bit down hard with his two new baby teeth.

"Ouch! That wasn't called for, William. I'm feeding you just as fast as I can. Did you see me take even one tiny bite? No sir, not one. But maybe I will, just to teach you some patience." Christine spooned a glutinous lump into her own mouth and William let out an offended roar. She choked the lump down her throat. "Don't see how you could even like this stuff. Without molasses and all."

But she continued to feed him until the bowl was empty. Hoisting him to her shoulder, she next cleared a space on the table and tended to his diaper. That might have been setting him off some, too.

William was now happy and wanted to play. Christine was not in a playful mood. She slung him back in his crib. When his expression turned furious with the realization of his abandonment, she gave him her old stuffed doll to fuss with and headed out front.

The wind slammed the screen door behind her as she searched for her parents. There they were, by the truck, trying to tie down the snippets and pieces of canvas still clinging to the skeleton Christine and her father had built on the bed. As fast as they had one piece settled, another whipped itself loose.

Christine was trotting over to help, hugging her arms to her body against the chill wind, when the hail started. It fell of a sudden out of the leaden sky, fast and hard. Wasn't any little pellets, either. Was big hunks half the size of a baseball. One hit Christine on the head and stopped her cold in her tracks. When more followed, she crumpled onto the hard dirt of the yard.

Christine woke up back in bed. Her mother was sitting next to her on a kitchen chair, knitting. Christine groaned as she tried to move her head. Felt like it was being pounded all over. It took a while to realize that the pounding came mostly from outside her head, not inside. She glanced up at the ceiling.

"Is it still hailing?" she whispered. "Is the tin roof going to hold up?"

Her mother's fingers stopped mid-stitch. "I don't know. About the roof. But yes, it's still hailing."

"What's happening to the world, Mama?"

"I don't know that, either, child."

Christine groaned again as she rearranged herself. Nothing but one big ache. That's all she was. She seemed to be back in her nightgown, too. How had that happened? And her legs felt funny. She pulled at the sheet to look, but her mother stopped her.

"I had to bandage you some. There may be scars."

"It's only my legs, Ma."

Slow tears were working down her mother's face again. Her cropped blond hair, shoved back behind her ears, was showing brand-new signs of silver at the temples, too. "Only your legs! What about the rest of you? What have you been doing to yourself?" She dropped the needles to fumble for a handkerchief. "What have you been doing to your brother?"

"We wanted to tell you, Mama. We truly did." Christine reached out to touch her mother's arm. It felt warm and solid. It was real. "Please, Ma, could I put my head in your lap?"

Her mother was already off the chair and on her knees by the bed. Her arms were around Christine, knitting and handkerchief forgotten. "I didn't want to force you, honey. The age you're getting to be, things start changing. Sometimes you need secrets . . . But not if they're going to hurt you. Not then."

"It wasn't ever anything but good, Ma. Until last night. It changed last night. Like the weather."

Her mother hugged her tighter. "What changed, Christine? What?"

"My place . . . *Our* place, Michael's and mine. The *cave*." Christine's tense body relaxed. There. It was out. She'd said the word. "It's so beautiful, Mama. We wanted so badly for you to see it. But we were scared, too. Scared your coming might change things. Not *your* coming, but Daddy's."

"Are you that frightened of your poor father?"

"It's not that, Ma. But I knew you would have to tell him. You tell him everything." She suddenly remembered last night's scene in the dark. "By and by."

"When a man and a woman love each other, Christine, they do that."

"Do they have to? Always?"

Mama was slowly caressing her brow, moving her fingers through Christine's hair. "If they trust and respect each other."

Christine sighed. She wasn't completely sure she wanted to continue growing up. Not immediately. Her mother's fingers lingered over their gentle massage.

"Tell me about the cave, honey. If you can. If you're finally ready."

Christine turned her head to search for Michael. He was rolled into a tight ball, asleep. "I found it, but I suppose Michael started it. I wanted so bad for him to get better. And the air's different down there, Ma. Down there, he can breathe."

Her mother's arms tensed. "What do you mean, he can breathe?"

Bit by bit, Christine began to explain. It took a long time. Every so often, her mother got up to fuss with baby William. He was still in his crib, sort of talking to himself. But he was happy with her doll. He'd already chewed off two legs and was batting them around in triumph. The arms would probably go next. Well, she hadn't really needed that doll anymore. Not for a long time. The hail began to slack off, to change into a lighter staccato.

"Where's Daddy, Ma?"

"Probably in the barn, licking his wounds."

"The hail didn't clonk him, too, did it?"

"No, Christine. Events have just gotten a little . . . beyond him. Tell me more about your crystals and icicles, dear. I can almost begin to picture them. It sounds so peaceful."

"It was, it is. At least until last night . . ."

Michael was still sleeping at suppertime. Christine ached, but got up anyway to set the table. Every so often, she stopped to glance out the back door. The sky remained gunmetal gray, but the wind had stopped. It was still cold and a slick layer of hail covered everything, just beginning to melt into itself.

"Can that stuff wet down the dust, Dad?"

He shrugged his shoulders.

"When it melts, will there be any seedlings left underneath?"

"Maybe. More so now than if the grain was taller."

"So it's not a total disaster?"

"Christine," her mother said from the stove. "Bring me your father's plate to fill."

Christine studied the segmented meat dropped onto her father's plate before she handed it to him. It looked suspiciously like skinned rattlesnake, even disguised with a thick brown gravy. "We run out of elk sausage already?"

Her mother shook her head. "It just seemed to me something different was called for."

They sat awhile at table, the three of them and baby William, staring at each other. Finally, needing to do something to cut through the heavy silence, Christine spoke.

"Would you teach me how to knit, Ma?"

"Knit? You never had an interest before, Christine."

"True. But there's lots of things you know that could be useful. Knitting could be useful of an evening. Give a person something different to think about. 'Course, if we had a radio, that might be useful, too."

"No electricity." Her father finally spoke two words.

"You can get 'em battery-operated, Dad, running on all these car batteries. I've seen them at the general store for sale. But I expect they cost more."

"Haven't got money for fripperies. Haven't got money period."

"Ernest, dear," Mama broke in as she hunted through her knitting bag for her extra set of needles. "Ernest, dear. You know how we always said we'd maybe make a little room out of the attic space, when the children got bigger? We said it from the start after we built the house, when your parents' place was hit by lightning."

Christine watched her father eye her mother like she'd clean lost her mind. We're *leaving*, his eyes said, clear as day. *Leaving* just as soon as the weather's better and repairs are made on the truck.

Mama ignored those eyes for once. "Christine's getting to be of a certain age. She'll be needing her privacy. We'll have to stuff the walls against the winter wind, though. And find another mattress for her."

Christine's head swiveled between her mother's words and her father's eyes. A room of her own, without Michael and baby William? A room to keep things in? Things that William wouldn't chew on, or tear apart? A room as private and completely hers alone as the cave had been the first day she'd discovered it? Christine accepted two needles and clumsily wrapped yarn around them in imitation of her mother. That might be something worth growing up over.

Christine seriously began to worry about Michael when she crawled back into bed. He'd been up once for a groggy run to the outhouse, but that was all. Straight back to sleep. Could he only be exhausted from the late nights and the wind and the excitement?

She settled back against her pillow. The other night she'd wanted nothing so much as to be alone. But did she want to be alone all the time upstairs in the attic? Wouldn't she miss whispering with Michael? Christine shrugged in the dark. Her own private room couldn't happen, anyway. Not if the rain didn't come. Not with the hail covering the dust which covered the barren earth. Her private room for a long time to come would be a few square feet of the truck bed, squished in between Michael and baby William. Squished in between Mama and Daddy. There wouldn't even be the distance of the kitchen curtain between the children and their parents. There'd be no space for private conversations with Michael. There'd be no stories. Most of all, there'd be no cave.

Christine got out of bed and groped for the counting stick. In the dark, her fingers slid over the marks, counting. She'd forgotten to mark today. Could hail be considered rain? Could that be the Lord's answer to the water she'd asked for? No. God couldn't be that mean, not after He'd gotten them out of the wind tunnel last night. Maybe the hail was just His way of telling her to be patient, telling her not to be greedy like baby William over his food.

Christine touched the last mark on the stick, then carefully scratched in another one with a fingernail. She'd gouge out the mark properly in the morning, when she added the new day's.

Christine woke to sunshine, heat, and a yawning Michael. He grinned at her.

"Boy, what a sleepyhead you've been, Chrissie. Seems I've been waiting the longest time for you to get up."

"You could have crawled over me if you were that hungry."

He felt for his stomach. It had filled out a little recently. "Wow! I am hungry! Hungry enough for a dozen elk sausages!"

Christine stared at him. "Are you all right, Michael?"

"Why? Never better—" He stopped. "Only, I just

remembered. We have to explain about the cave today, don't we? To Mama and Daddy."

Christine shook her head. "I already did the explaining to Mama. Yesterday."

"What do you mean, *yesterday*?"

"I mean you slept through the entire night after the wind. And the entire day yesterday. Then you slept all the way through last night on top of it."

"I lost a day? A whole day? What happened?"

Christine rubbed at her head where she still had several sizable lumps from the hail. "We got some precipitation, but not exactly the kind we were waiting on." She jumped out of bed. "Come on. Let's see what happened to the hail."

What happened to the hail was that it was gone. In its place was a thin layer of muck that covered everything in their gully and beyond. Christine swooped through the kitchen and out the door to squidge in it with her bare feet. She looked up at the sky. The sun was burning down so hard the mud was already starting to layer and crack across its top edges, like new ice on the river in winter.

Michael swept out the door behind her and slid clear through the stuff, skidding into Christine, to land stretched full on his side. He lay there giggling. "I think I made a home run, Chrissie."

"Michael!" Their mother was calling from the back

door. "Michael. I'm truly glad you're better, but that's the last set of wearable overalls you own. After what you did to your others in that, that *adventure* of yours!"

Michael sheepishly pulled himself out of the muck. Then he made the mistake of trying to wipe himself off. His hands came away as black as his pants. "Sorry, Mama. I guess I'm not used to mud. Only dust."

"Come eat your breakfast, children. It's eggs."

"Eggs!"

Michael dashed for the kitchen. Christine came more slowly. Daddy was letting them eat the eggs now, too. Usually he took them into town to trade for flour and such. At this rate, they'd be having roast chicken for supper. An image of succulent drumsticks with crispy skin passed through her mind, making her mouth water. The last chicken they'd squandered for roasting had been at Christmas. It was a curious price to have to pay for leaving.

Mama must not have said anything yet to Daddy about the cave. At least he didn't let on through the entire course of the morning, as Christine helped him to patch the truck canvas. When they finished with that, he stayed inside the truck bed, measuring spaces with her mother's dress tape. Christine watched him from a safe distance, then trotted after him into the house and watched again as he carefully measured the mattress and the table. Even the kitchen chairs.

Her mother watched silently, too, only interrupting

when he walked past the walnut dresser by her bed.

"What about my dresser, Ernest?" She touched the leaf carvings on its drawer lovingly.

Daddy shook his head. "Too heavy."

"But it's the only good piece we own, Ernest. The only piece saved from the house fire. It was Mother's and my grandmother's before that. *They* hauled it out by wagon clear from Ohio."

"We'll discuss it later, Clarise."

Daddy moved on through the curtain to the back bedroom. They heard him trip over something and give a yell. Christine rushed in to get a fix on the problem.

"Stones!" he was fuming. "What are stones doing in the house?"

Christine raised a hand to remove the offending object. It was too late. He slung it straight out the open rear window. Christine ran to the window to find where it had landed. It was one of the cave stones, after all. It meant something to her, and to Michael. It had helped get them through the wind. Daddy must have slung it with some force, for it was clear across the yard, up against a small boulder sitting there. And it had cracked.

"That was *my* stone, Daddy! It was important!"

Close to tears, Christine ran from the room and the house, straight out to gather up her cave stone. Michael beat her to it. He stood staring at the two halves, gleaming in the sun.

"Chrissie! It's got the cave inside!"

Christine stooped to cradle half in her hand. It was hollow, and the inner wall was lined with lovely purple crystals. Michael was touching the crystals of the other half. "Do we have to take it back to the cave?"

"I don't know, Michael," Christine considered. "It's already out, isn't it. As if it were meant to be . . . All this loveliness was hiding inside the cave. Down there, it was just a plain old rock. It couldn't give any competition whatever to your Christmas tree, or the icicles."

"Then it's all right?" Michael was beaming. " 'Cause if it's all right I'm giving my half to Mama right now."

"It might cheer her up at that." Christine smiled back. "But it would look much better with my half attached. We could put it back together, like an eggshell—"

Michael was already grabbing for Christine's half. "Won't she laugh when she opens it?"

And she did. Their mother smiled, then laughed, then began patting at the corners of her eyes. Daddy stormed in from the bedroom to find out what was so funny. He was stopped by the glistening brilliance on the kitchen table.

"It's a geode. *Amethyst*. Where the dickens did it come from?"

"From you, Dad," Christine smiled. "When you threw my rock."

He slumped into a chair and stretched a hand to

touch it. "Are there more? Do you know where to get more?"

Christine looked at her mother. Her smile had faded. I was right, Christine thought. Right as rain. And Mama knows it now, too. Tell Daddy about the cave, take him to the cave, and everything *would* be different. Everything about the cave, that is. Maybe the spread, too.

Christine knew it would not be a good kind of difference for the cave. She believed that as firmly as she was standing there on her own two muddy feet. But would it be another kind of difference for their home? Would it make a difference in their leaving? . . . Was the staying worth the changes?

"I asked you a question, Christine." Her father turned to Michael. "What about you? You have something to add to this?"

Michael shook a no dumbly, his mouth opening and closing helplessly a few times. Christine tried to save the situation, at least long enough to think it through better.

"We found it in the hills, Daddy." That was the truth, at least. "On our walks. Along with a few others."

Her father ruffled his thick brown hair impatiently before jumping to his feet, eyes snapping. "Those others. Where are they?"

Michael's eyes were welling up with wetness and frustration. Christine prodded her brother. "Go get them, Michael. From under the bed."

There were three more of the rounded stones that they'd hauled clear back to the house. They'd forgotten them after their escape. In their total exhaustion, Christine and Michael hadn't even felt the extra weight. Their father practically snatched them from Michael's hands and stomped out into the yard. Michael and Christine followed. Even their mother followed, carrying William.

Christine watched her father place the stones in the sun, then disappear into the barn. He returned with a hammer and chisel. He centered the chisel carefully on the largest of the three, raised his hammer, and gave the chisel one swift tap. The stone split.

This one was hollow, too, but there were no gleaming jewels inside, just a rougher gray coating than on the outside. Her father grunted disappointment, but Christine was glad. Glad this stone hadn't blossomed like their mother's. Maybe her father would calm down and not push her and Michael further. Maybe he wouldn't need to know about the cave. She watched him raise his tools to the second stone, her breath held. The hammer banged, the stone parted smoothly. Her father gasped.

Inside were pure, gleaming white crystals. They were lovingly formed, more extravagantly than their mother's amethyst. The last stone also bore true. From inside the cavity radiated rich, amber-colored spears, looking as if they'd been just waiting, bursting to be set free. Christine started breathing again. She might as well.

Holding her breath till she was blue in the face wasn't going to stop her father from any of the plans that were moving across his face, as easy to read as any book.

He glanced up at his family. "This might change things some. If there are more." He narrowed his attentions on the two children. "Are there?"

Michael refused to answer. He was working his toes again, this time without the boots. Christine figured Michael was aiming for more than the root cellar. More likely he was considering burrowing clear through the earth to China.

"Is there something wrong with what I'm asking? Is there, Christine?"

"I'm not sure, Dad. Could be a few more of those rocks floating around."

"*Geodes*. They're called geodes."

"*Geodes*. How'd you come to know that, Dad? About what they're called?"

"I did some prospecting in the Badlands, before I married your mother."

"You ever find anything?"

"Nothing worth giving up the farm for."

"Well, then, I guess this little bit of excitement oughtn't to be much different, either."

Daddy ignored Christine and got to his feet. "I'm taking these into town. I might be able to trade them for a few gallons of gas."

"Not Mama's!" Michael burst out. "You're not taking Mama's! That was a present!"

Daddy turned from one member of the family to another. "For the life of me, I can't figure why I'm the villain of a sudden." He paused. "All right, I won't take your mother's."

They watched him carefully cradle the crystals in the cab of the pickup. They stared as he started the ignition and slammed the door. He poked his head out the open window on the driver's side. "Maybe we'd better go with more elk sausage for supper tonight, Clarise. Give the brown hen a few more days to lay."

11

It was getting toward sunset and Mama was worrying whether or not to hold dinner for Daddy. Michael was of the opinion that they should eat without him. He was still feeling robbed. Christine wasn't sure how she was feeling. Baby William was definitely feeling hungry. He was pounding at the top of his high chair so lustily they almost missed the sounds of the returning truck.

Mama glanced at her amethyst crystals. Michael had defiantly centered them on the kitchen table, where the hill flowers had sat until every blessed petal had wilted and fallen. "These won't ever wilt on you, Mama," he'd said. Now Mama was concentrating on the crystals, wondering like everyone else. "He's home," she announced suddenly.

Daddy came into the kitchen boyish again, almost bounding, hands behind his back. "Got an entire tank of gas, and filled up the five-gallon can." He brought his arms forward. "I got these, too."

He proudly placed two shiny gallon cans on the table. Christine read the labels, though she didn't need to. *Molasses*, one said, and the other, *Blue Ribbon Lard*.

"Free and clear. All free and clear. At least on indefinite account. Al Hilmer said as how he'd take more of those geodes any day. Said he can sell them for a good price to that tourist shop in Hot Springs when he goes in for supplies and split the money with me."

Daddy stood back, waiting to be congratulated.

"That's nice, Ernest. Would you like your supper now?"

Christine watched her father sit, confused and deflated. She pried the lid off the tin of molasses and proceeded to pass it around the table. It did pick up the elk sausage, slathered on bountifully. At least, it picked it up as far as her mouth. Sliding down her throat, the molasses made her choke. Tasted bitter, it did. Tasted the same as she figured that gall tasted the Wicked had forced at Jesus on the cross. She gagged and reached for her water glass.

————

Earlier in the afternoon, after Daddy had taken off in the truck, Christine had confronted Mama. "May Michael and I walk out to the cave? I believe Daddy's staying-home days are almost legally used up."

Mama gasped. "You'd go back? After the wind?"

"I have to settle this geode business in my mind, Ma. You know Daddy's going to be after us when he gets home."

"Yes . . . I suppose you're right, Christine." She lowered her eyes to Michael. "If there's a wind, the bad kind, you don't go in. Even if it does help your asthma. That's an order."

"Sure, Mama. You couldn't force me, anyhow."

"Take your boots!"

Christine went into the house for their boots. She picked up several candles, too. She hadn't really planned to go back into the cave just yet, only to check those other rocks they'd left by the mouth. But if the wind was blowing the right way it wouldn't hurt to hunt for their lanterns. Outside again, she yelled for Michael to fetch two pails from the barn. He collected them and they headed over the hills, empty pails swinging.

"It feels sort of funny, Chrissie, going to the cave legal."

"Legal for Mama. Not necessarily Daddy."

Michael swung his pail some more. "Daddy ever sets foot in there, the whole place is likely to end up for sale somewheres."

"Looks as if he's proving that pretty clear. He wasn't always like that, either, before the drought."

"Before the drought was a long time ago, Chrissie. I don't remember a whole lot about then."

"Well, he was proud of the land. Proud to sell his baled-up alfalfa to the ranchers for winter fodder. We made enough to get by, he always said. He wasn't hungry for more."

"I don't know that he's all that hungry for more now, Chrissie. Just hungry for the way it used to be. For enough." Michael was beginning to stick up for their father, even if he had run off with the geodes.

Christine shrugged. "Maybe you're right."

They crept up on the mouth gingerly, afraid of what it might be doing. But it wasn't doing anything unusual. Just breathing out calmly.

"I think it's safe, Michael."

Michael, who'd carefully remained to the rear, wanted more time. "Let's check these rocks we left here first." He gathered them together and counted them. "Nine. And they all look about the same. That's why I picked them up to begin with. They weren't too rough for my pockets."

Christine carefully placed the rocks in one of the buckets. Nine potential geodes. How many would hold tiny caves? How many would be empty? She picked up the other pail.

"Want to try the cave, Michael? We don't have to if you don't want to. I thought maybe we'd just walk till we locate the lamps. I'm kind of curious to see how far we got before we found the string."

"You sure couldn't tell the other night." Michael edged up to the mouth and sucked up a deep breath. "It smells good again."

Taking another load of cave air into his lungs, he disappeared into the hole.

They walked steadily through the passageway, flashing their candles around the floor. It seemed a very long way before they found the kerosene lamp. Christine stooped to straighten and light it.

"We didn't get but a few yards from the big room, Michael. See? And it seemed like miles, like forever."

"It was forever, no matter what it looks like now." He ran for his own lamp. "My old candle's gone. Lucky we brought more."

They entered the cavern and swung their lights around.

"Gosh. Daddy's geodes. They're everywhere, Chrissie."

Christine was looking, too. "I know. We never saw them before." But here they were, scattered haphazardly nearly everywhere her eyes lit. Just odds and ends of stone rubble left over from the building of the rest of the cave.

Every time they came into the cave, they found, noticed, something new. If they had their entire lives to spend down here, there'd always be something new. If it weren't stolen first. Christine set down the pail.

"Shall I fill it, Chrissie?"

"Not yet, Michael. Let me think."

"You sure spend a lot of time down here thinking."

"It's important. And necessary. Especially now."

"Maybe we'd better head over to the water, then."

The stream had calmed. Christine knelt by the bank and sliced her fingers into the currents. She could still feel them, even if they weren't rippling the water. The currents remained strong right beneath the surface, single-mindedly making for the pond, the river, and the falls. They acted a lot like people, a lot like her father. Every so often, he stormed up, hissing and spitting. But even when he wasn't acting that way on the outside, the currents worked on underneath. He had a plan the same as the water. Either make it here, on his own land, or move on to greener pastures. Mama was one of the fish, swimming as fast as she could, just trying to keep up.

"I'm not convinced we should take too many of those geodes back home, Michael."

"Because of them leaving the cave?"

"That. And because of Daddy. If he thinks there's an endless supply tucked away somewhere—"

"But there is!"

"Wouldn't be endless for long, Michael. Anyway, if he thinks there's an endless supply, he's going to want to know its source. And no matter what Mama says about sharing, I don't think this information would help Daddy."

"But if he could trade them for stuff we need—"

"That's not how you felt earlier, when Daddy wanted to run off with Mama's present."

"That's before we saw how many there truly are. Besides, those were special rocks, even for geodes. Even the empty one. They helped save us."

"That's the whole point. Maybe the others are here for a special reason, too."

"Not to save Daddy?"

Christine shook her head. "It's the wrong kind of saving, not the kind he needs. He just as much as said he wasn't cut out to be a prospector. What he is cut out for is to be a farmer—a good one, too, when the rains come the way they should."

"I don't think Daddy'd appreciate your figuring his life out for him like this."

"No. He probably wouldn't. But this cave, Michael" —she spread her arms to encompass it—"it's bigger than all of us. Grander, too . . . I don't think it was meant to trade for gasoline."

They went back with the nine stones split between the two pails, Christine carrying the heavier one. She could justify those nine stones. They were already out of the cave for a legitimate reason. She still couldn't force herself to justify disturbing the others inside.

The next morning Christine frowned at the counting stick. Only four days left and no rain. But maybe the hail could be counted as something. It had tamped down the dust. There was even the faintest tinge of green to the unburnt hills this morning.

Her father had noticed, too. He was standing in the middle of the yard, speculatively examining the hummocks rising and sliding around them. He'd built their house as far down in the gully as he could get between those hills. He'd done that as a windbreak, against the regular north and west winds, the same as his father had. Other neighbors, without such a gully, or not wanting the closed-in feeling of it, had built their houses right out on the level. Then they'd planted rows of trees to the north and the west, to the same purpose.

If Christine had any money, she'd spend it planting rows of those trees, hills or not. There was something comforting about trees. Maybe it was their greenness. Always green, even in the drought—if they didn't flat out shrivel and die. Also, trees could be climbed. Wouldn't that be something. To climb a tree right here by the house and be able to see miles over the plains in all directions. Maybe even as far as the cave.

"Christine . . ." Her father's voice pulled her out of her thoughts.

"Yes, Dad?"

"These hills don't look like geode bearers. Buffalo grass, yes. Geodes, no. The geology isn't right."

Maybe he hadn't even noticed the greening. It was starting again. "What's geology, Dad?"

He frowned sharply. "I'm not putting up with any of your leg-pulling. Yesterday was enough."

"Wouldn't pull your leg, Dad. It was a serious question. You know my education's been interrupted these last few years. Seems to me if you've got a stock of educational information, least you could do is share it—"

"Christine!" His face was redding up again under the tan. She watched him struggle hard with the anger. His better self won, at least for the moment. "It's a part of science. It deals with the history of the earth. Through rocks."

"You can read history through an old rock?"

"Old rocks *are* history."

"Like George Washington and Abraham Lincoln and—"

"You're trying me badly, daughter. Where did you and Michael find those geodes?"

"Just where I said. Floating around the hills. Be pretty hard to pin down an exact spot . . ." It would, indeed. They'd picked them up helter-skelter inside their big room. Before they knew better.

When he spoke again, her father's voice took on a

tone she'd never heard before. A begging, pleading tone. "I need more, Christine. Can you begin to understand that?"

She shook her head. "You don't, not truly. It's something for nothing. Something for nothing never settled anything. You didn't even notice the hills greening, did you? Just thinking about something for nothing. If you were your right self, Daddy, you'd be hooking Big Ben up to the plow and making some rows for Mama's garden. Then I'd plant seeds and we'd have something real. Something to work for."

Her father took two steps in her direction, his hand raised. Christine stood her ground. He'd never struck her in her entire life. Not even once. He stopped, and the arm lowered.

"Your mama was right. You are going through a change. I pity the man ends up with you in a few years."

"He'll have to be a strong man, Daddy. The way you are when the alfalfa's growing."

Christine turned away. Maybe she'd just hook Big Ben to the plow herself. What had caused her to sass her father like that, anyway? She couldn't figure it. Just a few weeks back, she'd have waited there, head down, toeing the ground like Michael. She'd have handed over those nine geodes hidden in the barn, too. She could have done that now and smoothed everything over. But she didn't feel like smoothing everything over. And she didn't feel like giving up the cave. The way she was feeling, she'd let herself be eaten up by lions, like the early Christians had, before she gave up that cave. God's hand was in that cave sure as it was mostly missing out in these hills right now. Giving up the cave for barter would be sacrilege.

Christine felt a sudden twinge in her back, and in her stomach, too. Must be all that elk sausage creeping up on her. She went off to catch Big Ben.

Michael straddled a fence post, watching her work for a while, handing out free advice. She'd been right earlier. Anything that free was sheer useless.

"Jiggle the leads a little. Show Big Ben who's boss! . . . More to the right, Chrissie. You got a curve there bigger than the bend in the Cheyenne . . . Get to the end of a row, usually have to bribe Big Ben with a fistful of grass to start him into a turn."

Christine let up on the plowshare, picked up a clod of hard earth, considered her action carefully in her mind, and slung it at her brother.

His arm came up defensively. "Hey! No call to attack me thataways."

Christine selected another clod and tossed it in her hand, up and down a few times. Michael got the message and slid off the fence to go annoy the chickens.

Sweat was dripping all over her when Mama yelled out to stop for the noon dinner. Christine unhooked the mule and tied him to a post near the water trough so he could help himself when he was good and ready. That done, she examined the fruits of her labors. Half a dozen crooked rows. It wasn't as easy to follow a plow around as it looked. She stooped to inspect the earth she'd turned, picking up a handful to run through her fingers.

The hail hadn't done all that much. There'd been a little moisture near the top, but a few inches down, the soil was rock-hard, crumbling to dust with the stirring. Maybe six rows were enough. Six rows she could almost water from the trough. At least until the seeds got a start. Daddy might fuss about using up their water, but when the rain came, it would surely fill the well again.

"Your meal is getting cold, Christine!"

"Coming, Ma."

Christine swallowed a full glass of water, then stared at the elk sausage on her plate. Mama had fried it in lard, and the grease had congealed while she tarried. Her stomach turned. No eggs. No chicken. Her father must still be harboring hopes of ferreting that geology information out of her. *Geology.* It had a nice ring to it. She wished suddenly that she had a book about geology. It might answer a lot of her questions about the cave. Then again, Daddy might be able to answer a lot of those questions, too. He might even be able to put names to things. If she were ever to ask.

"Eat your meal, honey. You must be starved, taking on Big Ben and the garden the way you have this morning."

"No offense, Ma, but I'm really not hungry." Christine pushed the plate away. Her father looked up for the first time from his own plate and speared her sausage with his fork.

"We're not rich enough to be wasting good food."

Christine watched him methodically work through her sausage. Even that gave her a queasy feeling. Where had he gotten his appetite? He hadn't even been plowing. She put her head down on the table.

"Christine? You need a nap, dear?"

"Maybe I do, Ma. I must've gotten too much sun this morning."

Christine felt worse after her rest. She stumbled out into the kitchen clutching her stomach, to collapse into a chair. Her mother looked up from the table where she was cutting apart a ragged pair of Daddy's overalls to redesign for Michael.

"What's the matter, honey?"

"I feel terrible, Ma. All crampy, and headachy, and a backache, too."

"Oh, dear. I was hoping you had a little time yet. But you are almost thirteen."

"A little time for what, Ma? What are you talking about?"

Her mother got up to check out the back door. She came back to sit down. "Michael's playing with the baby, and your father is off doing heaven knows what. Probably nothing. He's so in between things with himself, poor man."

"About my stomach, Ma. I thought at first it was just more elk sausage. But I didn't eat any at lunchtime—"

Her mother fussed with the scissors and finally put them down to touch Christine's hand. "It's not that, daughter. It's about becoming a woman." And then she began haltingly to explain.

Christine listened, forgetting about her pains. When her mother's tentative recital was finished, she was aghast. "Every month like clockwork for practically the rest of my entire life?"

Her mother nodded.

Then Christine got angry. "That's not fair! Not fair at all!"

"Life isn't, always. Besides, you get used to it. After a while, you hardly even notice."

Not notice all this discomfort? "What about boys? What happens to them? What's going to happen to Michael?"

Her mother hesitated. "Well, not nearly anything like this."

"What do you mean!"

"Don't yell, dear. It isn't comely." Mama waited for Christine to simmer down. "Men are different. When they grow up, they have to shoulder the burdens of their families. They're responsible for their support."

"You help with that, too."

"True." Her mother searched for other justifications.

"Then there's war. In times of war, it's the young men who have to go off to fight."

"We're between wars, Ma. There was the Revolution and the Civil War, and then the Great War to End All Wars. Miss Cleanthe Smith explained a little about those."

"Miss Cleanthe Smith was fairly busy during her short stay, it would seem." Mama picked up the scissors again. "I think we're still between wars. I haven't seen a newspaper for so long, though, anything might be happening. The last I read, there seemed to be troubles in Germany again."

"That's in Europe, isn't it? And Europe's a fair distance from South Dakota—all the way across the country, then across the ocean, too. My cramps are here and now, and the thought of them being responsible for another baby, like William, isn't too heartening."

"The cramps aren't responsible, dear. It takes a husband first."

"And that's years away. So why couldn't they hold off?"

Her mother shoved some loose hair behind her ears. "It's just nature's way, Christine. That's all I can say. Seems to me I felt a little like you when it first happened to me. You get used to it, though. You have to."

"I wish I was a boy. Wish I'd been born a boy. Wouldn't have to put up with all this nonsense. Wouldn't have to put up with a lot of other nonsense, either."

Mama leaned over to give her a hug. "Oh, honey, I've wished that on occasion, too. But *I'm* happy you're a girl. And we women have to stick together. We can do things men can't do. We can feel things they can't feel. Sometimes I'm sure God made flowers just for us. To make up for everything else." She focused on her amethyst pushed to the side of the working space. "Sometimes I think everything beautiful in the world is for us, because we see it differently from men. I wouldn't want you to miss that."

Christine grumbled under her breath before speaking up. "Flowers aside, I might be needing that attic room sooner than any of us anticipated."

12

In the end, it was Mama herself who went to the barn to beard Daddy about the attic room.

He was confused. "Already? It can't wait?"

"It can't wait."

He hauled in the shorter hay ladder and poked open the trapdoor in the back-bedroom ceiling with it, lodging the ladder in place before disappearing outside again. Christine and her mother teetered up with the broom and rags and a bucket of soapy water. Supper waited that night until they had scrubbed the dust from everything. And, even before supper, Mama made

Daddy drag up the top mattress from Christine and Michael's bed.

Michael was bewildered. He sat on the hard springs left to him in the back bedroom and bounced, once. "What's going on?" he yelled up the ladder. "And why does *she* get the mattress and I get the springs?"

In sympathy, baby William whined from where Michael had plunked him in his crib. Their mother edged down the barn ladder carefully. She wiped her face, leaving a streak of dust two inches wide across it.

"It's just time, that's all, Michael." She wiped her hands next, adding to the soot on her apron. Then she picked up a quilt and spread it evenly over the springs. "There. That will make it softer for the moment. I'll dig out my winter comforter from the hope chest after dinner. Tomorrow we'll see about fixing up something better for you, Michael."

There certainly had been a few surprises hovering around *this* day. And for once hadn't any of them been about the cave. Christine lay on the mattress in her huge new room considering them. The bed felt funny without Michael squeezed in next to her. Too big somehow. She wasn't used to being able to stretch out and not contact a warm body. Wasn't even used to being able to stretch out.

Christine tried for it, tentatively. She inched out her fingers, then her hand, finally her arm. She thrust out her legs in both directions. Space. Endless space, and darkness, too, like in the big cavern. No icicles, though. But they might creep in with the winter. If the rain came and her family was still here.

Christine lay stretched out full for a while before curling into a ball again. Who'd have thought her body had surprises in it as mysterious as the cave? And Mama had said it wasn't all bad. Had nearly promised. Christine slowly uncurled again and began painting flowers and crystals with her mind all over the blackness of the attic surrounding her. If the change had to come, she sincerely hoped there'd be some beauty attached to it, inside and out.

Michael was grumpy at breakfast.

"I couldn't sleep proper at all last night." He reached a hand to his back. "I ache all over from those hard springs. And there wasn't anybody to talk to." He glared at his sister.

Christine toyed with her oatmeal. She still wasn't hungry, and she still couldn't face the molasses. "You can help me plant the garden this morning, Michael. The way you promised. It'll take the creaks out of your back."

"When did I promise? I never promised such a thing!"

"Michael. Collect yourself enough to remember a few weeks back. With the stick."

Their father reached for the molasses. "What stick? And I'm not sure I want you wasting the seeds. They'll never come up without water."

"I'm planning to water each and every row until the rain comes, Dad."

He plunked down the syrup can. "The rain's not coming and I'm not wasting any more time with your nonsense. Either of you. I won't have you squabbling over the garden and I won't have you making up any more tales about your geodes. I have something else in mind for both of you today."

Christine caught her mother's glance across the table. Had she told her father about the cave? Had he finally wheedled it out of her? Her mother made a little movement with her head. No. Mama hadn't worked out the moralities yet, either.

"What did you have in mind, Dad?"

"I thought we could take a walk in the hills. Just the three of us."

"You going to give us some nature lessons, Dad?"

"What I'm going to give you is the tail end of my belt, young lady, I don't get some cooperation!"

"Ernest—"

"Don't *Ernest* me, Clarise. Your children have been getting too big for their britches, and it isn't natural growing I'm referring to."

"Just let me throw in a few seeds, Dad, before we go? You'll feel much better, seeing something sprout green."

"Nothing is going to sprout green on this land ever again. And I'm not wasting any more time on it. We're walking in the hills today. Tomorrow we're packing and leaving."

Daddy threw his spoon on the table and stomped out. Christine stared at her bowl.

"Well, at least that's only one more night on those rusty springs."

"Michael! How could you ever feel that way, after everything—"

Mama got up from the table. "Where did you leave those marigold seeds we saved, Christine? I might just plant a few while you're gone."

Christine kicked back her chair and ran around the table to throw her arms around her mother. "Ma. Oh, Ma. What do I do about the cave?"

"You'll have to use your own mind, daughter. But your father's not going to be worth living with till he gets to the bottom of the thing."

"It's bottomless, Mama. It's—"

She tipped up Christine's chin. "That's not what I was meaning. You know it." A kiss was dropped on her daughter's forehead. "Better be taking your boots and sweaters, just in case. And don't go over-exerting, either. You should be easier on yourself for a few days."

"I never see you going easier on yourself, Ma."

"That's different. I'm used to it."

"What are you two going on about?" Michael remained querulous. "And do we have to take Daddy to our cave?"

Mama shook her head and got them out the door.

The wind was hushed, dead quiet for once. But the sun was hot. Christine plodded slowly behind her father and Michael toward the west. Daddy had taken that direction automatically. He'd seen them disappear that way too often. Maybe they should've been covering their tracks better all this time. That was it, Christine thought to herself. They should have taken off for the east sometime, or even straight north, then worked their way around to the west. They should have used cunning. But they hadn't been the least bit cunning, and now it was too late.

Her father didn't even need to be led once they'd gotten over the first hill. Track marks from Michael and her travels had made a path through the blackened grass. A straight path clear to the cave. Why hadn't she noticed that before, either?

Stupid. She'd been stupid and unthinking. Her legs slowed even more. She stopped to wipe her dripping face on her arm and to massage the small of her back where it still ached with this growing business. Even if she turned into the most lovely flower imaginable—which was hard to imagine—even that couldn't make up for losing the other beauty of the cave. Even if—

"Christine!"

"Yes, Dad?"

"Pick up your feet. Dawdling isn't going to change anything."

He was probably right. She arched her back, groaned, and moved forward.

When her father got to the spot where they'd found the elk, he paused. He studied the burned grass at his feet, then the green meadow above, before returning his eyes to his feet.

"I never noticed this piece of land before. Not properly. Acts as if it's got water under its roots. An aquifer?"

"What's an aquifer, Daddy?" Michael finally found his voice. He'd probably been having second thoughts about this enterprise, too.

Their father answered without barking, thoughtfully. "A patch of natural underground water. Water that's always there, even in drought. The kind of thing you hunt for when you're after digging a well."

"Oh." Michael bit his lip. He knew as surely as Christine that there was no aquifer under that hill. Not unless you counted the stream running through their cave, which *was* water.

Christine's stomach began to sink as her father shrugged and moved on again, starting to round the last hill before the mouth. Why had he needed them on this walk, anyway? He'd asked for no directions. He'd gone straight along their well-worn path. And in a moment he'd be at the opening. At their secret cave.

In spite of herself, Christine ran forward. She wasn't sure what he'd say or how he'd act. She had to know.

In slow motion, her father circled the last hill and ground to a halt. Christine and Michael skidded behind him, almost into him. There were their lanterns, where they'd left them. They'd had their hands full of pails on the last trip. Not that either would do much good today. The kerosene lamp was nearly empty, and Michael's candle was melted to a nub. There stood the mouth of the cave, set into the soft, grassy cliff, opening into its black hole.

"So that's what became of my rope. I'd nearly forgotten."

It was all their father said as he studied the rope knotted tightly around the boulder before it snaked into the hole. He turned to consider his two children for a long moment. Finally he picked up a length of the rope and walked to the edge.

Christine closed her eyes and prayed. Michael clung to her wordlessly. Maybe his eyes were closed, too, trying to make believe this wasn't happening. They both opened their eyes fast enough when they heard their father's grunt.

Michael was poking at Christine. "The wind, Chrissie!"

"Yes." Christine smiled beatifically. Their father was flat on his bottom two yards in front of the hole, clutching at the shirttails ripped clear out of his overalls. "The wind changed again."

An hour later, they were still squatting in front of the hole. Every five minutes their father had tested the wind. If anything, its sucking vehemence increased, while the air around them, the outside air, became stiller and heavier.

He spoke, almost to himself. "I never would have believed it. That wind must be pulling a hundred fifty miles an hour. We won't get down there today." He finally noticed his children. "It can't always be like this. It isn't, is it?"

Neither answered.

"The geodes. They came from down there. Didn't they."

Christine replied at last. "It's just a little cave I happened on, Dad. Nothing to get excited about."

"Nothing to get excited about. Just a little cave on my land . . . I think it's still my land. Rasmussen pays me a few dollars a year grazing rights on it . . . I never bothered doing a proper survey, though. It never seemed necessary. I had enough to farm down by the river . . ."

"You still do, Dad."

"What's that?" He'd continued talking out loud, more to himself than to Michael and Christine.

"You still have enough to farm down by the river."

"Stop taunting me, Christine! You know the land's

nothing but powder, and the river, too. You can't farm powder! When will you get that into your head?"

"We haven't had a dust storm in the longest time, Daddy. And the hail dampened things. We might even have ended up with some fine Nebraska topsoil. Also—" She twitched her shoulders as a rivulet of sweat ran down her spine between them. Wouldn't it feel good and cool in the big room by the stream right about now. Wouldn't that water taste wonderful. "Also, things happen when the wind sucks in from the mouth."

"What do you mean, things happen?"

"Last time the wind changed, Daddy," Michael broke in, "last time—"

"—it hailed," Christine finished.

Their father poked his head into the opening yet again, and was almost swallowed yet again. This time there was a smile of understanding on his face. "A barometer," he mumbled. "Could be a natural barometer. And if it's blowing that hard . . ." He dragged himself away from the wind and focused his attention on the sky.

Hadn't any of them paid the sky any mind for the entire hour they'd been hanging on outside the cave. Christine swung her head up, too. It was different. There were clouds now, out of nowhere. Strange, swirly clouds, moving fast.

Their father gave both children a shove. "Home! Get home fast!" He swooped down for the lanterns and began to run. Christine and Michael lingered a long moment, not understanding.

"What's the matter, Dad?"

"Move, you two! That's a twister forming!"

A twister? Christine had only heard about such things. There hadn't been one in her memory. But what she'd heard made her legs move of their own volition. Twisters swooped down out of nowhere, wreaking paths of incredible destruction.

She forgot her aches, she forgot the deadening heat. She forgot everything except to keep moving, and to make sure that Michael kept moving in front of her. Their father was already well ahead. He'd be worrying about Mama and baby William and Big Ben and the chickens. And getting the trapdoor open to the root cellar.

Halfway home, Michael crumpled to his knees, thoroughly winded. "Haven't got any more run in my legs, Chrissie," he gasped. "I just haven't."

Christine sank down for a minute, too. "Take your time. Breathe slowly." She chanced a look at the sky. It had gone angry black and all those tortured clouds were forming into a curious funnel shape. Through the heaving of her chest, she could even hear it moaning. "Then again, forget about breathing. We don't move out, that twister's going to fly us home on its tail, all by itself."

Christine grabbed at Michael's nearest arm and

forced him to his feet. Half running, half stumbling, they covered the remaining hills. When they got to the one above their home gully, they just slid over and rolled down the last side. As she rolled, Christine's eyes caught brief glimpses of that giant funnel writhing and swirling maddeningly. Wind whistled around them nearly worse than in the tunnel of the cave that other night.

Lying flat on her nose at the bottom of the hill, Christine tried to dredge up enough strength to make the last yards to the house. Somehow she couldn't find it. Chaos busting loose around her, her mind settled instead on the calm of the vast cascade room, the golden lights glowing over the river's cataract.

Out of the wind, of a sudden, strong arms snatched at her. They tucked her on one side, Michael on the other. Strong legs carried the two into the house, straight down to Mama in the root cellar. The trapdoor banged shut.

"I'm sorry, Daddy." Christine fainted in his arms.

13

Christine returned to consciousness in the root cellar surrounded by the whole family. Mama had thought to bring blankets and Christine was swaddled in one, still lodged in her father's arms. The lantern from the kitchen table was flickering from an empty shelf, casting dim light over other shelves that lined the hard dirt walls of the small, cool room.

Christine stared at a lone jar of tomatoes. There used to be about fifty of them sitting there. Right underneath, that's where the jellies and jams had been. They'd finished up the last one—strawberry—round about Easter. The next shelf down, that used to be for the beans and pickles. There were two jars of three-bean salad remaining. And the root bins themselves, why they'd been empty for months, too. All except for the handful of sprouting potatoes that her mother had hung on to in hopes for the kitchen garden.

Baby William was sleeping in Mama's arms, scrunched right atop Michael's head resting in her lap. Michael didn't seem to mind, as he was sleeping, too. Mama's eyes had been closed, but now they opened.

"Are you all right, Christine?" She kept her voice soft and low, so as not to wake the little ones.

"I think so, Ma." She wriggled to get more comfortable in her father's arms. "It was awful nice of Daddy to save Michael and me the way he did. After the bad time we've been giving him."

Her father's arms tightened around her. "In God's name, Christine! Did you think I didn't love you?"

"It was hard there for a while, Dad. Not being absolutely sure."

His grip almost began to pain. "There's nothing on this earth more precious to me than your mother and you children."

"Not even the land? . . . Not even the geodes?"

She felt the sharp intake of his breath. She could feel it all the way through his chest, past his stomach, and up to his heart.

"It hurts me to watch you all going without. Without proper food, without even *lard*. Not butter, *lard* . . .

To listen to Michael cough . . . What good is the land if I can't even keep my family healthy and fed? What good am I? I can't take you into town because you haven't decent clothes. Can't buy you a radio . . ."

Christine listened to the wind pummeling the house above them, howling like an entire tribe of Indians on the warpath. It was scary. Eerie. Directly above her head, the trapdoor rattled and shook as if the fingers of wind were trying to personally break into her family's sanctuary, to capture and scalp them once and for all. To finish up the job the drought and the dust had begun. Christine shivered. Would their home still be there when they poked their heads out of the cellar? Would her new room still be there? It might've been fun decorating it the way it had looked in her mind last night.

"I don't need a radio, Daddy. Don't even need new clothes. I just want you and Mama to be happy. As happy as Michael and I were down in our cave." Another blast hammered at the trapdoor, then sloughed off with a scream of frustration. Christine relaxed within her father's grip. She felt him begin to breathe evenly again. "Daddy?"

"Yes?"

"In a cave, what do you call something that looks just like an icicle hanging down? But it's stone. Hard stone."

"A stalactite. You call them stalactites. Icicles coming up from the floor you call stalagmites."

"Don't have any of them. The stalagmites. At least

we haven't found any yet, Michael and I." Christine closed her eyes and drifted back into sleep.

The kitchen was still there when Daddy decreed the trapdoor could be opened. He went up first, carrying the lantern, leaving the others in darkness. Christine could see him swing the light around, searching out trouble.

"Seems to be clear," he called down.

Mama handed up baby William first. Next she pointed the sleepy Michael at the steps. He grabbed onto the railing and pulled himself up. Christine followed, her mother completing the rear.

In silence they glanced around the room. It had been some wind. Chairs were toppled, even frying pans were slung around, mixed with shards of broken window glass. The flour canister had been tossed and there was a trail of white powder around the floor. But the ceiling was still intact. Daddy went outside to see about the roof, and Christine followed.

She was surprised that it was still day. Late day yet light enough. The sky had cleared, but a heavy humidness hung like a veil over everything. Everything. Christine took in the buildings. The roof of the house was there, all of it. And the tin, too. It made a neat "A" over the front of the house. She turned. The barn stood firm, but the outhouse had been lifted and set down again, three yards from its foundation. The henhouse was lodged shakily on its side, two hens perched atop it. It was all the same, her world, yet changed, slightly askew. A sudden bray of terror rang through the evening, shaking her.

"That's Big Ben, Dad. Got to be. Didn't you get him safely into the barn?"

He shook his head, trying to pin down the mule's location. "There wasn't time. He and the hens had to fend for themselves."

The mule let out another bellow, this time of outrage, and they both jumped. Why Big Ben was upset was that he was perched smack atop the canvas on the rear of the truck. All four hooves had broken through the cloth and he was slung there, suspended on his belly.

Christine and her father stood in the fading light, staring at him unbelievingly.

"How'd he get on top of the truck, Dad?"

Her father shook his head. "Twisters have done stranger things. More to the point, how do we get him down?"

"He must've been knocked out and just came to. Like I did. Do you think he's hurt? I'd hate to have him hurt, Dad."

"I don't think so. At least he wasn't wearing any harness in the field. That could have caught on something, maybe choked him." Her father stepped back another few feet to better evaluate the situation. Coming to some sort of decision, he moved into action, hoisting himself under the canvas into the bed of the truck.

Christine followed slowly, wondering. Big Ben had been in the north field, nearly a quarter mile from the buildings, nearly a quarter mile from the truck. They'd been moving him around a good bit lately, hoping fresh fields—even if parched—would fill his stomach while he wasn't working. That big funnel of wind had just picked him up bodily, dropping him when it grew tired of the game. Dropping him smack atop the canvas of their truck. She didn't want to think of other places it could have dropped Big Ben. She especially didn't want to think of where the twister might have dropped her and Michael if their father hadn't rescued them. She closed her mind to the idea and scrambled into the truck.

It was a rare sight, watching four disembodied legs hanging down from the canvas and pipe covering they'd built. Christine touched a foreleg, hoping to calm the poor beast. It got him more frightened than ever and he began lashing out in all directions. Daddy just missed getting clobbered. He jumped back, rubbing at a grazed arm.

"There doesn't seem to be anything wrong with his legs. But I think I'd leave off with the sympathy till we've got Big Ben safely down."

"Good point, Dad." Christine backed off a safe foot, just to the tailgate, and thought about how they'd have to do it. They'd have to dismantle the entire contraption, pipes first. When they let the pipes down, Big Ben would come down, too. All they'd have to do then was to cut him out of the canvas and walk him off the truck on a ramp. He'd be good as new. As for their covered wagon . . . Christine laughed right out loud.

"I know this is an unusual situation, young lady, but I fail to see the humor in it."

"Why not, Dad?" She was still laughing, and it felt good. "That twister and Big Ben both are telling you something. Telling you this covered wagon was never meant for heading farther west."

"Get me the pliers and a wrench and something to cut with, Christine. The lantern, too. It's getting too dark to see in here. We'll assess the damage after we've saved the mule."

Big Ben was in the barn, laying into an unexpected feast of warm mash. He'd been rubbed and loved until he acted as if he didn't want to see another human for a good while.

Michael had finally woken and chased down their chickens in the dark. Amazingly, they were all present and accounted for. Angry, but accounted for, though they'd probably be off egg production for a few days. They were a mite leery of their henhouse, too, even though Daddy had taken a moment from appraising other damage to shove it back on its bottom.

The fat brown hen had been huddled just inside the unhinged door of the outhouse. They'd found her last, after they'd dealt with the mule. Daddy picked her up by her legs and handed the squawking chicken to Michael. Then he considered the outhouse itself.

"I guess we'll have to hitch the tractor up to it tomorrow. Get it back on its moorings. I don't like to leave without things being shipshape."

Christine said nothing. Even knowing about the cave hadn't changed her father's mind about the leaving. That should have made her feel better, but it didn't. She'd purposely made the cave seem unimportant, except for that stalactite business when her defenses were way down. It wasn't unimportant. It never could be. Christine deserted her father for the kitchen. Mama had managed a pot of coffee and a pan of cornmeal mush in between picking up the mess.

"We haven't found the screen door yet, Ma," Christine remarked as she collapsed into an upright chair. All this business with the weather and saving Big Ben was exhausting. "But Daddy thinks he may have enough sheet glass lying around the barn to fix the kitchen windows. He wants everything in order before leaving. I guess that's so when the rain finally comes it won't destroy your kitchen."

Her mother slid a plate of the mush in front of Christine and pushed over the molasses can. "You may as well eat, honey. It doesn't look as if we'll be doing it together tonight." She sank down across from her daughter and stared at what remained of her kitchen. Surprisingly, the Hot Springs calendar still fluttered from its nail on the wall. "It doesn't seem as if anything's going to change your father's mind, does it."

"Nope. Not even the cave." Christine frowned at the untouched molasses and took a dry bite. "How he plans to rebuild the back of the truck again, though . . . Well, that beats me. Big Ben really did it in."

"He'll be up most of the night trying. To keep to his schedule."

"It won't get done by tomorrow, Ma. I can promise. Daddy'll have to hold off another day yet." And tomorrow would be two days before the counting stick was used up. What if she were to bribe her father with the geodes still hidden in the barn? What if she were to walk him back to the cave and show him the other geodes when the wind was blowing the right way? Would it be blowing right tomorrow?

Everything came back to the cave. All the questions, all the answers—about the weather, about her life. How much could she give up, how much could she save? Absently, Christine reached for the molasses and poured some over her cornmeal.

14

When Christine woke in the morning, she ran to the ventilation slats where the roof gabled in the front of her room and poked at them until they grudgingly opened an inch. She'd dreamed of rain again. It was the old dream, so real that she'd nearly believed it.

Plastering her eye to the opening, she was momentarily blinded by the rising sun coming over an eastern hill. Directly in front, to the south, a stream should be forming in their front yard, if it had really rained. It should be sweeping across a muddy dirt road, down over her father's alfalfa fields, directly into the Cheyenne River. Christine squinted. No. It wasn't a river again. It wasn't all frothed up and excited with somewhere to go. It hadn't rained. Her eyes came back to their own yard and stopped near the barn.

Her stomach sank. Daddy was fussing with the back of the truck again. Still. Christine ran for her clothes and slid down the ladder. She raced right past her mother in the kitchen and out to the truck.

"Daddy!"

He looked up, his hands filled with mangled canvas. "What is it?"

"Why are you messing with the truck?"

"Gotta keep my options open, Christine."

"You have to have more faith! There's still two days! We have to plant the garden. We have to—"

"And what will we eat while the garden is growing —if it grows? You saw those shelves in the cellar. Bare."

"Not bare. Only nearly."

"Are we going to live two months on one jar of tomatoes and two of bean salad?"

Christine was taken aback. She hadn't been the only one counting. "There's the elk, Dad. And more in the hills." She stopped. "And there's the cave."

He dropped the canvas and stared at her. "All these weeks you've been hiding it. Now you're finally ready to take me down?"

Christine swallowed. It was hard. "If it could make

things different for you, for us . . . It's just that it's special, Dad. More special than I let on. It doesn't like change. It doesn't want to be . . . *robbed*."

"I thought we'd worked out a few things last night, Christine. Now I'm a thief?"

"No, Dad." This time she was hanging her head. It had come out all wrong, her offer.

"And this cave of yours. You make it sound as if it's alive."

"You felt the wind yesterday, Dad. You saw it talking to us. Talking to you. It made you see the twister. It *is* alive."

He jumped off the truck. "We'll eat breakfast. Then we'll give your cave one more chance."

Michael came along with them. He insisted it was his cave as much as Christine's, and if anybody was going to give it away, he ought to be part of the giving.

Daddy still hadn't understood. "It's on *my* land. How do you two come to figure it's *your* cave?"

"It's been on your land for years, Dad," Christine let out before thinking. "But the cave never made a present of itself to anyone but *us*, Michael and me."

She waited for him to get all hot and bothered about that, but he didn't. He just kept plodding on, wiping the sweat from his face. They came to the hill where they'd shot the elk. They went round the next one. They stopped.

"Chrissie," Michael hissed.

Christine grabbed at her brother, hanging on to him for dear life. It couldn't be. But it was.

The cave was gone.

At least, the opening was gone. Where the mouth had glared blackly was nothing but a crumpled hillside. Crumpled with tons and tons of dirt and rocks and boulders from above the cliff.

Her father backed away, total despair etched on his face. "It was the twister."

Christine backed away, too, then let go of Michael and collapsed onto the blackened grass. It was all she could do. Her legs had just given out under her. The cave had made up its own mind. It had chosen not to be violated. It—or God—had made the final decision. Beside her, Michael started to cry. Christine couldn't cry. She was too dried out, too empty.

Alone in her bed that night, Christine tossed and turned for hours until the tears finally came. They came heavy and hard and blended with another sound that she never even noticed. Not until the morning.

Exhausted, tear-stained, Christine crept down the ladder and into the kitchen. Her mother was standing by where the screen door ought to have been, staring out into the yard.

"What is it, Ma?"

"You haven't noticed? Come and look, honey."

Christine rubbed her eyes and looked out into a gray

world of soft, steady rain. Rain. She thought she'd been cried out, but more tears came. *Rain.* Right on schedule, pretty much. She ought to have been out there dancing in it, but somehow couldn't.

"Is this going to change Daddy's mind?"

"I'm not sure, Christine. I just don't know."

Christine walked into the rain, barefoot. The dust had already gone squishy under her toes. She kept walking, feeling the mud begin to cake around her feet and onto her ankles. Her father was standing just inside the barn door, staring out at his truck.

"Will it be enough to save the alfalfa, Dad?"

"I'm not certain. If it keeps up gently like this . . ."

"Yes?"

"A hard rain would carry off all the loose topsoil. If it just stays easy, there might be a chance."

"We wouldn't have to leave, then?"

He shrugged. "Find us something to eat in the meantime, daughter, and then I'll be able to answer you."

Christine walked past her father, directly to Big Ben's hay pile. She burrowed in it until she'd found the rocks, all nine of them. "Dad?"

"What is it?"

"I've found us something to eat."

They waited till Michael was up to crack open the geodes. Even Mama came through the rain with baby William to watch. Daddy tapped them open in the dim light at the entrance of the barn, one by one. There weren't any duds. Each and every geode held a crystal miracle.

When he was finished with the work, Daddy stepped back. "Christine?"

"Yes, Dad?"

"Pick one out for yourself. You, too, Michael."

"You don't have to do that, Dad. It was a free-will gift—"

"Hush up, Chrissie," Michael burst out. "*I* want one!"

Christine smiled and bent to make her choice.

Michael wanted to examine hers, and as she let him, he whispered in her ear. "Ever think about there being another opening to our cave, Chrissie? Somewhere for the wind to come from? Maybe near the waterfall?"

"I don't see why there couldn't be, Michael. How about we start hunting directly after the kitchen garden is planted?"